Haunted By

Demons

The Irene Martinez Story

By Irene Martinez

Copyright © 2017

ISBN: 978-1-9999220-0-9

First Edition
Mrs. Irene J Nunez Martinez

And there was war in heaven. Michael and his angels fought against the dragon, and the dragon and his angels fought back. But he was not strong enough, and they lost their place in heaven. The great dragon was hurled down–that ancient serpent called the devil, or Satan, who leads the whole world astray. He was hurled to the earth, and his angels with him.

Revelation12: 7-9 "NIV" Holy Bible

Acknowledgements

I would sincerely like to thank the following people for their help in the completion of this book.

I would like to thank my son Jose Nunez Cole, who spent a lot of time and effort in creating the cover for the book and also help with the editing of this book for Print and Digital Ebook.

I would like to thank Dr. Graham Clingbine for his help in proof-reading my book. Also for supporting me as a fellow author and friend.

From the Holy Bible New International Version 'NIV'

Hodder & Stoughton

Peter 5: 8-9-10-11

Luke 11: 24-25-26

Revelations 12: 7-8-9

Jeremiah 29: 11-12-13

Contents

Introduction

Preface

Introduction

This book is a true story from my own experiences.

I'm Irene Martinez I was born in Norfolk and around the age of two I moved with my parents to live in East London. I began my studies in theatrical training at the age of six which was the beginning of my dream to work in show business. I studied a number of different dancing styles including tap dancing, modern ballet and Spanish dancing. Also studied singing and acting and went on to work at the age of twelve in Pantomime each Christmas. This continued throughout my teenage years while I continued my school studies.

From 1960 I went on tour with two different circuses. One circus was in Portugal and the other one in Spain. After I got married I continued working as a solo specialty dance attraction with my own variety shows and then as a singer with my husband's band touring around Europe and the Middle East. During those years I met many statesmen and royalty in various countries in which I worked and visited while travelling around the world.

During the 1980's my issue of demonization began to surface while I was working with one of my shows in Turkey. After that period I remained mainly working in England. Although my health wasn't good, I still found a variety of different jobs. I worked as a manager in a number of shops and ran my own theatrical agency along with doing promotional work in many major stores.

From the 1980's my life radically transformed and gradually turned into a living state of hellish suffering daily with the condition attacking my body, which gradually engulfed my whole life. However, I still continued to search for help to resolve my problem of living with the condition. During those years I saw many different people from the church and also a variety of other people with different remedies which helped but didn't resolve my problem.

While I was on this journey, I discovered after visiting a well-known psychic college that I was a natural 'sensitive' with the gift clairvoyance (clear vision) and a form of clairaudience (clear hearing) that many mediums have. I never studied or wanted such gifts. They came to me from out of the blue and made me an easy target for spirits or demons to contact or attack.

Hence my time in Turkey heralded the start of my demonization as the demonic stronghold took up residence inside my body. I've spent years trying to get rid of this horrific condition and have continued searching to find my Holy Grail of peace and deliverance.

In 2006 I began to receive the teachings coming from the Holy Spirit. These continued for a number of years and during this time I continued to suffer both physical and mental torments from demonic attacks. Due to these experiences the birth of my first book 'Trials Torments and Teachings' came into being that's now published.

Today I am still battling on and fighting every step of the way to be freed completely from the condition. I hope my Holy Grail of deliverance is close to ending my ongoing nightmare. I hope you enjoy reading this book Haunted by Demons which is the full story of how my supernatural experiences began and overtook my body and life. I've had to cope and live with these issues over the years since the 1980s up to the present time

Preface

Before my experience with the supernatural world of horror began, I'd read a few articles about the subject in magazines and newspapers and also about people who'd experienced strange ordeals of the supernatural type. I never took what I read too seriously until it happened to me. Although many strange paranormal stories have been made over the years into films or TV series, I never dreamt that anything of this strange nature would ever touch my life. However, it did during the 1980s and created upheaval in my career and life at the time. I had thought that such events were fantasies until inexplicable happenings started to affect me in Ankara. I guess I'd just been too complacent about the paranormal world and now I was about to learn that it existed as it gradually began to touch my life. Its evil clutches began to grasp at my body revealing the first wake-up call of its existence.

Devastating effects began to engulf my normal working life in show business at that time. Once the condition began it gradually took over my whole life which turned into a chaotic state. I was going to have to learn to adapt to live with this for many years. When the voices first began I thought it could be a form of transferring information through telepathy as I'd seen a program about this on TV which also included remote viewing which America was testing and already using. This was one of the ideas I had when my condition first began and I heard voices. Another one was that it might be a radio being played softly somewhere in the hotel that I was hearing. It wasn't either of these but it was the start of my demonization. The demonic spirits began to attach themselves to my body and this was the start of my endless horror living with them at close quarters.

Chapter 1

The Fatal Journey

I'm feeling slightly phased today as I take my mind back in time to Ankara and begin to remember how my supernatural encounters first began taking place during the 1980s from which I've suffered ever since. I open the curtains of the back room and notice the sky's a dark grey with heavy clouds forming as the first drops of rain fall and beat against the windows.

The storm begins with a heavy downpour of rain followed by a loud clap of thunder. The back room I'm in turns gloomy as I sit down at my desk and open my computer and begin to type my story. Who knows why these strange supernatural incidents take place in people's lives to destroy them. My encounter began taking place gradually and led up to the demonization of my body which has continued to linger on throughout the years with its aftermath up to the present day. Mine's a strange true story that unfolded into my life without any warning, which I've been forced to live with ever since. That's what led me to take the decision and write this book.

It all began during the early summer months of the 1980s when I was working on a contract in Ankara with my show. From that time onwards a strange unknown dark energy began entering my life that's remained with me over the passing years. The condition has turned my whole existence into a never ending nightmare that I can't wake up from. As my story is a true one I want to give a clear picture of what actually happened to me in Turkey once these supernatural manifestations began taking place. During the months that I was working there as I became demonized with the condition that's far worse than being struck by lightning. When it takes place in your body and life. The effects of it are dangerous and have been drastic for me to live with. In this book I've included many of the weird and frightening incidents that took place during the years that I've suffered with this condition. As this is a horrific ordeal for anyone to bare. Being held a hostage by a demonic spirits turned my life into an oppressive bondage. This is the outcome of having to live with demons residing inside my own body.

My prison sentence began from the moment they came into my world and it has lasted for half of my lifetime. How can I explain what a hellish state this condition brings for a person? Once the demonization came I could see my life disappearing rapidly through the turmoil it brought. I became a prisoner battling on through each day to survive and keep my mind intact. I had to keep strong as more unclean spirits gradually came to join the network of demons and attach themselves to the outside of my body and mind to torment and abuse me.

The seeds of my story were sown when I wrote to an agent in Turkey for work with my new production show. A reply came with an offer for a job from Mr. Macy in Turkey, to whom I'd written while I was working in Holland over the Christmas period. His offer was a six month contract to start work in Istanbul. When our job came to an end in Holland we returned to England and started rehearsing for the next few weeks while we waited for the visas and tickets to arrive. Eventually everything came and we left for Turkey in the middle of January and flew from Heathrow to Istanbul. I didn't realize at the time that this was going to be the most 'fatal' journey that I'd ever take when I accepted that contract. It was going to take me into the realms of darkness and a paranormal world of spiritual warfare that was going to change my life forever.

We arrived in Istanbul and were meet at the airport by Mr. Macy, our agent, who informed me we'd be starting work in a couple of days at one of the largest Casino's in the center of Istanbul. I felt quite excited being back in Istanbul again as the place always held a certain air of mystery about it.

When you walked through its streets with the vendors lined up to sell you their wares it felt like they were woven into a tapestry of time with Istanbul's culture. I'd worked in Istanbul several times over the past years and the atmosphere in the streets always gave me a feeling of uncertainty about what might lie around the next corner as you walked through them. My daydreaming was cut short when the transport arrived that Mr. Macy had arranged to take us to our hotel. By now it was late afternoon as we drove across town to reach our hotel

The mosques we passed on our journey stood tall against the skyline captured in the rays of winter sunlight which turned them into a golden glow. We reached our hotel as the sunlight was fading in late afternoon. Dusk was descending upon the streets as we were ushered into the lobby of the hotel where I would be staying. The rooms were sorted out and I got my key, took the lift and went up to my room which would be my base while working in Istanbul.

As I started unpacking my cases I had a weird premonition that something was going to happen that would change my life on this trip and the feeling clung to me. Was it just a figment of my imagination working overtime or was something sinister really going to take place? I turned my thoughts back to the show and felt pleased that Mr. Macy had found a good venue for us to start work in the Casino. My show was a production one with lots of glamour, beautiful costumes and plenty of feathers and glitter. This was the type of show that most of the Casinos wanted during the 1980s. I hoped our show had the right image to draw in the public being a strong variety show with a handsome male dancer for the ladies in the audience. The musical score for the show was mainly from the Hollywood musicals and suitable for any type of audience.

On the opening night in Istanbul everything went well and the show looked spectacular. After all the rehearsals we'd done in England with the girl dancers, the presentation looked very glamourous with the dancers dressed in silver lame costumes with plenty of large white and pink plumes. Their hats were large and decorated with sliver sequins along with their back packs. The whole effect looked stunning under the rotating white spotlight. Everything on stage turned into a shimmering silver glow of moving stars.

As the dancers did formations around the stage with their large net fans covered in silver sequins. The glittering formations the dancers made looked fantastic against the dark interior walls of the Casino. Looking back now on that night so long ago in Istanbul, the rehearsals to prepare that show had taken a few months but the final result had been a good one. The show was well received and applauded by the audience that night. I did a few routines in the show with the dancers and performed my own specialties of tap dancing and singing as well.

Another favorite production number in our show was Tales from the Arabian Nights that looked very authentic with beautiful costumes. This was an all-round success with the audiences in the Middle East and brings back many happy memories of my years working with shows around the world. My husband made all the costumes for our shows and I designed quite a few of them. The oriental costumes turned out to be quite amazing and captured the audience's imagination when the dancers stepped onto the stage.

My own costume looked very much like what you might imagine Shahrazad wearing [from the tales of the Arabian Nights] when she told the Sultan her stories to stay alive. The costume was made of gold lame elaborately decorated with gold and red stones and my headdress was a large gold turban with a long veil covered entirely with stones and sequins. The costume looked beautiful under the stage lighting. We used some authentic Turkish music and some modern style that got the audience clapping and enjoying the routine. The show closed with a grand finale of feathers, diamantes and plenty of glitter as most productions shows had at that time.

The contract in Istanbul was cut short after we'd worked at the Casino for about three weeks. Mr. Macy called me to say we'd be moving onto Izmir for a five week contract. I felt confident about returning to Izmir as I'd worked there before during the 1970s. Until Mr. Macy arrives with the transport to leave for Izmir, there's someone I'd like to tell you about who returns back into my life in Ankara and this story. Then a strange chain of events started taking place as my nightmare began to materialize in Ankara.

I'd worked in Turkey several times over the years and in the 1970s I accepted a contract to work in Izmir with a new show that I'd just formed in England. To get the job in Izmir I'd gone through the usual procedure of writing to various different agents to find work. I waited for a couple of weeks and then the first offer of a contract came through an agent that I'd known for many years from Turkey. The contract gave me the chance of a further three months prolongation for the show if the club liked us. If they didn't prolong the contract I'd planned on going to Greece

When the agent called me in England to say that he'd found a three month contract for Izmir which would give him plenty of time to look for other jobs for us, I agreed and signed the contract. We waited for several weeks until the work visas and travel arrangements came. They finally arrived with our date of departure for Turkey.

Chapter 2

Izmir the 1970s

It was early January when we left for Turkey and the weather was cold and damp when we arrived in Istanbul off the plane. Our agent Mr. Macy was waiting at the airport to meet us and informed me that we'd be travelling down to Izmir that evening by coach. The Club we were booked to work at were waiting for us to arrive and start work immediately. After spending a few hours in Istanbul we left that evening for Izmir by coach. I left with my eight dancer's, six costume trunks and about twenty six private cases which belonged to the dancers and myself.

The luggage caused quite a fuss when the coach driver and another man started loading it onto the coach. Then a great deal of screaming and shouting took place to achieve this task before we could finally board the coach ourselves. Then there was more fuss to get my group onto the coach and seated. The whole scenario gradually grew into a full scale drama to do this until we were all finally in our seats and ready to start the journey that lay ahead down to Izmir.

I guessed right away it was going to be a long tiring overnight journey to Izmir. The only information we got from the coach driver as we were leaving Istanbul behind in the distance was that we would arrive early next morning. Our journey began with a thunderous storm which continued on throughout the night with torrential rain that beat down onto the roof of the coach until the early hours of the morning. I knew when I got onto the coach it was going to be an uncomfortable long trip. I kept my mouth shut and didn't complain as it would cause an avalanche of moaning from the dancers. They were concerned why we hadn't gone by plane. The reason was it would have cost a lot more money for the club to pay with the amount of luggage we had. I kept my thoughts to myself as I glanced around the interior of the coach. Everything appeared to be well worn and shabby from years of use. The upholstery of the seats was a faded red color and various seats were torn in places and very hard to spend a long journey sitting on.

Most of the windows were dirty and rattled as the coach moved. Many of them were damaged as well and didn't shut properly. My observation turned out to be true and during the journey the rain poured in through the damaged windows. What can I say? We had a rough night on our journey to Izmir. Rain never stopped gushing down onto the coach and through the windows and I was sitting next to one of them and getting wetter by the hour. No wonder I ended up by the end of the journey looking like a drowned wet rat. We did stop a couple times on the way for drinks and toilet breaks going down to Izmir. When this took place we all had to do a runner through the rain to get to the cafeteria or the loo! I'd worn a smart black coat to travel in so I'd look presentable on arrival the next day.

When I finally got off the coach the following morning I had mud-caked all over my coat and shoes. My long hair was hanging damply around my face and my nose was bright red from the cold. I wasn't a very glamourous sight to see as we got off the coach. The dancers from my show were all tired and completely pissed off and grumpy from the overnight journey. They weren't doing their show business smiles either that morning but instead they were all moaning and complaining about what they'd gone through overnight as they got off the coach. It had been a long tedious night travelling through the storm with the atmosphere in the coach being humid and unbearable. The odors coming from the bodies and feet made it stifling to put up with. On that journey I kept praying silently to myself for it to end as the hours drifted by. I attempted to sleep several times but found it impossible in the cold damp odor-filled atmosphere. Early next morning the coach finally swung into Izmir's coach station and came to a halt. We'd arrived! It took some time to remove the luggage from under the coach off but the waiters who'd been sent from the club did that.

Once that was done and loaded onto cars we were taken to the hotel where we'd be staying while we were working in Izmir. On arrival at the hotel we were met by the manager of the club who was waiting for us to arrange the rehearsal time for the next day and to sort out the hotel. My first impression of him was a good one which turned out to be accurate. He was of the older generation and maybe in his late sixties with grey hair that was cut very short with a slight curl in it that matched his droopy moustache. His height was about 5'9 and he had a slightly bent posture when he walked. The manager's face was an interesting one that was well worn through the trials of life he'd experienced. What stood out were his eyes. They had a brilliant blue tint that toned with his hair. When he spoke it was with a soft broken English accent that could be easily understood. Breakfast was ordered for us all in the lounge of the hotel and paid for by him. We were then told to get some rest and settle in at the hotel.

Next day the waiters arrived at the hotel with transport to take us to the club for rehearsals. Working for this manager was like having a type of father figure in charge. The atmosphere at the club was always a comfortable and relaxed one with all the staff. After a good night's rest we rehearsed and started work the next day at the club. And we gradually got settled into a daily routine over the following weeks. Also, we got used to seeing the usual crowd of people on week nights and the ones that only came in at the weekend to see the show. We'd been working at the club for about a month and I was feeling quite comfortable about how things were going with the show and management. The hotel where we were staying at was close to the shops and not far from the club. Everything seemed to be working out ok in Izmir.

Generally at weekends the club was very busy and we usually had to do two shows on Friday and Saturday nights. On this particular Saturday evening I went out into the club just before the show was about to start to see if many people were coming in that night. The club was nearly full with still more people arriving. My dancers had already gone to change for the show and I'd got my tights and dance shoes on so I could be ready within minutes for our show. There were also several acts on before us so I had plenty of time. I was standing behind the stage curtains in the semi darkness of the club watching the people coming into the club.

The orchestra was playing a medley of music that they did every night before the show began. From where I was standing I had a good view of everyone coming in. The tables were all gradually taken and the club was full. The waiters were now all being kept busy going between tables taking orders for drinks and food. I stood watching this busy scene going on from behind the heavy dark curtains that surrounded the stage. Suddenly I noticed quite a fuss going on with a group of well-dressed men who had just arrived. By their gestures I could see that they wanted to sit at the two front tables which were already taken. The waiters seemed to know these people and were standing around the group of men talking to them intently. I gathered that they must be regular clients who spent quite a bit of money when they came into the club. That's why they were getting so much attention from the waiters.

One of the waiters went over and spoke to the people who were sitting at the two front tables and from what I could gather they were being asked to move to other tables. Quite a commotion and an argument went on until the task of moving them was finally achieved. Then the group of men who'd just arrived were then taken to the front tables and the other people were moved to different ones while still protesting. I continued to watch this drama being played out through a small gap in the curtains waiting to see what the outcome of this situation would be. It could have ended up turning into a fight. If this happened the show would be going on much later and the police would be called. Fortunately nothing happened and the whole commotion quietened down and the waiters began taking orders again. Peace returned once more to the Blue Moon Nightclub.

I remember that night clearly and being introduced to Tarik for the first time He was sitting at a front table facing the stage during our show that night. Ladies, you couldn't help but give Tarik a second look! He was about 6ft tall with an athletic appearance and a dominant personality which I'd noticed earlier that evening when he argued his way into getting the two front tables. He was the type of man who wouldn't budge until he'd achieved his goal. Now the waiters were busy arranging the two tables for Bossy Boots and his friends. While this was taking place, he took a chair and sat down with a transfixed gaze watching the waiters prepare the tables with fresh white cloths and flowers. Before long, a medley of music from My Fair Lady heralded the start of the show.

Bossy Boots was smoking a cigarette now and sitting at a central table facing the stage. He was definitely a very attractive man that you'd notice in a crowd. On that evening he was wearing dark colored slacks with a smart summer shirt open at the neck and a dark jacket. As I was watching him he took off his jacket, put it over the back of his chair and then glanced at both tables with satisfaction. As he did this I noticed he was around 40 as his hair was streaked with silver grey and cut very short. He looked tanned with sharp clear features. When he turned around slightly his eyes had the look of a strange translucent blue color from where I was standing. That was my first impression of Tarik. On that evening after our show we were invited to sit with his group. That's when I found out that he had a very charismatic charm that he could turn on and off in minutes.

At this point I was still behind the stage curtains watching him when suddenly he turned around and looked in my direction as if he could sense someone was watching him. I knew he couldn't see me as because I was well hidden but an eerie feeling came over me that he knew he was being watched. After the show that night the boss came around to the dressing room and asked me if the whole group would like to join the front tables for drinks and dinner as they'd like to invite us all. He then went on to reassure us that he knew these people well and that we wouldn't have any trouble with them. They were business men from Ankara who were in Izmir for a few days and this didn't happen very often. I spoke to the members of my show and they agreed to accept the invitation. Once we'd all changed into evening clothes the boss went with us to join the tables. As we were introduced to all the men in the group we found out that they all spoke good English and that most of them had been educated in England or America.

The waiters arrived with champagne and asked us all if we'd like dinner. The boss suggested we should have something to eat as the food would be specially cooked for us. All the men in the group were polite to us during the rest of the evening and the manager remained with us most of the time. When I was introduced to Bossy Boots I found out his name was Tarik and he thanked me for allowing my group to join his table and complimented me on the show saying he was surprised to find one like mine working in Turkey. Before the group of men left the club that night they all said they'd enjoyed meeting the group and the evening they'd spent with us at the club. Tarik mentioned he hoped to see us again next time he visited Izmir on business and left with the other men. I could see the boss was pleased with how the evening had gone as the men had covered our salary easily and spent quite a lot of money in the club that night.

Tarik came into the club again about six weeks later one evening with a friend and a further time on his own. Tarik dated one of my dancers a couple of times but always insisted that I join them when he came into the club, which made me feel awkward and like I was acting as a chaperone. He always asked me to sit and talk with him although the other dancers were already with him. I'd just done two one-hour shows when he came into the club. I was exhausted as I'd just finished the second show and I wasn't always good company to sit and chat with. This never bothered Tarik even if I was grumpy and silent. Money also never bothered him. He just wanted to sit and chat with the group and myself. Over the months his visits for business in Izmir became regular and quite frequent. I never had any problem with him and neither did any of my dancers. They all got on well with Tarik. He was intelligent company and a good conversationalist on most topics. Then one particular evening he arrived out of the blue again with another large group of his business associates just in time to see our show. Tarik asked one of the waiters to go into the town center and buy as many flowers as the shop could supply.

While we were on stage doing one of the routines in our show, the waiters started putting flowers all over the stage which left us no space to perform in. This could have caused an accident through the water of the flowers dripping onto the stage. When I saw what was happening I asked for the flowers to be removed. The club was full of people as the waiters started taking the flowers off the stage not realizing that by having the flowers removed from the stage Tarik felt insulted. This lowered his self-esteem and importance in front of a club that was full of people that night. He'd probably bought the flowers to impress me but I couldn't risk my dancers slipping and having an accident. So I stopped the show and announced over the microphone that it was very kind of the front table to send us so many flowers and I hoped that they'd forgive me for having them removed.

After the show that evening when my group joined Tarik's table as usual there was a very tense atmosphere. Tarik kept his calm exterior expression when I spoke to him about the incident. He apologized to me saying he was sorry and that he hadn't wanted to cause an accident by sending the flowers. I said it was a lovely thought and we'd all take some flowers back to the hotel with us. I thought that was the end of the story but it wasn't! After I'd spoken to him about the flower incident Tarik suddenly called the waiter and ordered about thirty bottles of Champagne which no one was going to drink or wanted as it was late and nearly closing time at the club. Nobody in my group or myself drank more than a glass or two at the most so I didn't understand why he'd ordered such a ridiculous amount of Champagne? When the waiters arrived with the bottles of champagne, Tarik asked them to open them all. He suddenly started throwing the champagne all over the stage and then came up to us all. He wished us goodnight and goodbye and left the club with his business friends.

I never saw or heard from Tarik again in the 1970s. Then he unexpectedly walked back into my life in Ankara in the 1980s. I'll have to stop my reminiscing now as Mr. Macy has just come through the main doors of the hotel into the lounge where I'm sitting.

"Hello Irene! You don't have much time as you're leaving this evening with your show for Ankara by coach. I've already bought the tickets and made the arrangements for transport to take you to the coach depo. Are you packed and ready to go with the dancers and costume trunks done? Everything's done and I was just waiting for you to tell me if we were travelling or not today?" That evening we left Izmir as the shadows of night descended upon the streets along with my past memories of the 1970s. Our journey to Ankara began when we boarded the coach with all the local people in the coach station in Izmir. We carried with us eight costume trunks, thirty-five personal cases of the dancers and myself. I felt slightly sad as our journey began to Ankara and we left Izmir behind in the distance. I knew this time it was forever. I sat back in my seat and let my thoughts drift about what lay ahead for me and the show in Ankara.

I had no premonition of what was about to take place in Ankara. Or of the experiences that would last for half of my lifetime to ruin my health and life. That would begin to take place soon after Tarik appeared back in my life when he came into the club where I was working one night in Ankara. From that moment on my life changed into a roller coaster ride into a world of supernatural darkness and oppression. That's when my endless nightmare began which would devour my life until the present time.

Once the demonic stronghold came they're manifestations and meddling through the voices changed everything completely. Which all started after I met Tarik again when our paths crossed in Ankara. You might say Tarik became a pawn in a game being played by demons who were using us and our lives. Maybe we were doomed to meet for the second time around on life's unpredictable journey. From then on everything changed drastically for me with my career in show business and with my family life. It all began with that fatal journey to Ankara where the walls of the Magic carpet were waiting to capture me into becoming one more Tale from the Arabian nights with Shahrazad waiting for me to add my strange weird story to her list.

Chapter 3

Ankara in the 1980s

Be self-controlled and alert. Your enemy the devil prowls around like a roaring lion looking for someone to devour. Resist him, standing firm in faith, because you know that your brothers throughout the world are undergoing the same kind of suffering. And the God of all grace who called you to his eternal glory in Christ, after you have suffered a little while, will himself restore you and make you strong, firm and steadfast. To him be the power for ever and ever Amen. Pet 5: 8-9, 10-11 Text "NIV"

We arrived safely in Ankara and were taken to the hotel which was situated in the center of town quite near the club where we would be working. Early the next morning I met Mr. Macy and the manager of the club in the lounge of the hotel. It felt like *déjà vu* as everything seemed to be repeated with the same scenario. Mr. Macy greeted me. "Good morning Irene." By his abrupt manner I could see he was in a hurry and wanted to get the business with the club over quickly so he could catch his afternoon flight back to Istanbul. I put my coat on quickly and joined both men. We left the hotel to walk down to the club. During the walk the club the manager didn't stop telling me how fabulous his club was and that he only catered for the best type of clientele. This was the reason why he'd booked us after seeing our show in the Casino in Istanbul as the majority of people came into his club mainly for the floor show.

I felt confident now that I was in the right place for this contract as my show was a good one with plenty of variety and suitable for this type of club. On that day as I walked into the club

I'd no premonition of what was about to take place over the next few weeks in my life. We arrived at the club and it looked presentable from the outside with a sign   Magic Carpet above the entrance door. There was a slight wait while the manager searched for the keys of the club in his coat pocket. He found them and opened the heavy outside door of the club. Mr. Macy held the door open for me to go through and I followed the manager down a flight of stairs that lead to another door. Now the three of us were still standing in semi darkness until this door was opened that led into the night club. Now complete darkness until the manager turned on the lights. When he did we were standing on a large floor area that was the stage where my story would begin to materialize over the coming weeks in Ankara.

Behind us was the usual bandstand for the musicians but what caught my attention right away were the walls of the club which were all painted with Tales from the Arabian nights. In the middle of one of the paintings there was a figure of a woman who might represent Scheherazade. Here comes the weird bit! She was wearing a costume similar to mine that I wear in the oriental routine. If she does represent Scheherazade most of her life was spent on death row if she didn't tell the Sultan a story daily. I just hoped this contract didn't turn out that way too.

I wonder now if my casual remarks on that day had tempted the realms of darkness for my story to materialize. I remained transfixed for a few moments looking at the figure and her strange resemblance to myself. It left me wondering if she had existed or just been a figment of someone's imagination. The imprints and strangeness of that day gradually began to unfold into my life. I don't know why felt slightly hypnotized gazing at the walls with their vivid paintings of the Arabian Nights but the spell of them captured me. My thoughts suddenly came back to the here and now when I heard the managers voice saying "what time do you want rehearsals tomorrow Irene?" I replied ''let's make it 2 pm with an orchestra call as well.'' Everything went ok with rehearsals and we started work the following evening at the club. For the next few days no big catastrophes took place with the dancers. I knew my job well and the pressures of managing a show and looking after the dancers while we were abroad. Yes, it was stressful sometimes and hard to cope with looking after other people's daughters.

Pin back your ears because it's Ground Hog day again! My strange story started one night in Ankara at the club. I had gone out into the club to talk to the orchestra about some music in the show. While I was doing this I noticed a group of men arriving that the manager and staff seemed to know. The whole scene reminded me exactly of Izmir in the 1970s. Was it the same group of men from Ankara? My life at that moment was like the film Ground Hog day and being repeated. I dismissed the idea and went to get changed for the show. That night I'd been right, it was Tarik making his second entrance back into my life. The stage was now set for my story to begin.

There was nothing unusual about Tarik spending an evening with business friends in a night club or casino, it was part of his lifestyle. When he came into the club where I was working that night it was just by chance, not planned. This was now turning exactly into the film Casablanca with Humphrey Bogart when he walked into Ingrid Bergman by accident! I'm not boasting, maybe Tarik heard there was a good show on at the Magic Carpet where we were working with a variety show with beautiful dancers. Here's the irony of the story. When Tarik walked into the club that night the band was playing Endless Love which sounded like the beginning of a perfect romantic story. Don't count on it, this one turned into a horror one instead.

That night when I was changing for the show in the dressing room, Bossy Boots was settling himself in with his friends around the usual two front tables. Snap! He was totally unaware that he was about to enter a strange morbid tale that would haunt the rest of my life forever. This was going to materialize over the next few weeks and would change my life into an unreal world. I was soon to begin living between two different worlds. I never realized what Tarik's entrance back into my life was about to bring. That night the show went alright so I was surprised when I heard a sharp knock on the dressing room door. I opened the door to find the club manager standing there who said in an urgent voice ''you've all been invited to the two front tables.''

My first reaction on seeing the manager was that he'd come to complain about something in the show and I was relieved to find it was only to invite the group. He grinned adding that the two front table had already placed an order for ten bottles of champagne. I knew this would cover his expenses for our show that night with a good profit. I repeated to him that my contract was only to do the show. He looked at me sheepishly and replied ''you and your dancers are all such lovely ladies, that's why everyone wants to invite you.'' At this point the money sign lit up in his eyes as he smiled at me. This manager was no different from all the others that I'd worked for over the years in thinking about how much money he could make that evening. I spoke to my dancers and let them know what the manager wanted. They accepted the invitation provided we all sat together as a group. I told the manager that my dancers had agreed to accept the invitation instead of going back to the hotel after the show. While the dancers worked for me abroad on contract, I was responsible for them during that time and for their safety.

After the discussion, we all changed into evening clothes and accompanied by the manager, went to join the two front tables that had now been placed together so there was plenty of room for my group. On our arrival we were introduced to all the men who were seated around the table busy eating and drinking apart from one man who was talking to one of the waiters. Suddenly this man turned around and stretched out his hand to shake mine, it was Tarik. While he was still holding my hand I looked straight into his piecing grey eyes and they twinkled with amusement. He made out that he didn't remember me. In today terms you might say he'd pressed my button and annoyed me and enjoyed doing it. That evening Tarik was dressed in a well-cut dark suit with a white shirt unbuttoned at the collar with no tie and looking his usual attractive self. He was full of confidence that evening and out to impress his business guests. It felt strange repeating the same scenario again three years later in Ankara. He was like a ghost from the past reappearing again by some strange plan of fate.

On that evening the seal of my fate was broken with the snare and trap in place as the doors of a supernatural world opened up into my life. This seemed to take shape after Tarik appeared back in my life. I never dreamt of meeting Tarik again but fate makes some strange entrances and exits in people's lives. From then on I seemed to have an unsettled feeling that something was about to happen but what? A few weeks later after that meeting and the trip to Zelve, the doors of hell opened up into my life. When this took place I was transported into an unbelievable world of voices, invisible trials and tortures over the following weeks, months and years. Both Tarik and I were placed on a chess board with our lives at stake, as pawns in a game of spiritual warfare. The demon gangs were waiting for us in the shadows of the night to begin their treacherous games with lies and deception.

I'm back in the club on that evening again listening to one of Tarik's long conversations that seems to last forever. It was difficult having to pay attention to what he was rambling on about and stop myself from going to sleep. I felt like telling him to shut up! At that moment he leaned towards me and gave me a smile and wink saying he'd never forgotten Izmir and the happy times he'd spent with me and my group.

After that the compliments flowed about my new show which he'd enjoyed and also about my professional ability as an all-round entertainer. Then he smiled at me adding that it had been enjoyable evening for him being with me again. I didn't mention that I was Mrs. Wonderful at my job too, as that might have ruined his evening. Thinking back over the years, he was one of the most confident people that I've ever met during my years of travelling around the world. Before he left the club that night he invited the dancers and myself out for lunch at a later date saying that he'd call me in a few days to arrange a day when he had some spare time.

The first few weeks in Ankara passed by quickly working, sleeping and rehearsing each day with the show with nothing out of the ordinary taking place in our everyday lives.

A few days after we'd sat with Tarik in the club he phoned me to say he'd like to invite the whole group out for an evening meal and would get back to me again to fix the evening. I spoke to the dancers and they agreed to go on the dinner date. It would be a treat eating somewhere different instead of our usual restaurant. Tarik rang me back a few days later and we arranged the evening. On that day we finished rehearsals early and went back to the hotel to get ready for the dinner date. We waited around the hotel for a couple of hours and Tarik didn't turn up. Eventually we got fed up waiting and went to our usual restaurant around the corner.

I never saw or heard from him again until he strolled into the club a couple of weeks later one night. He came over to talk to me as though nothing had taken place and never mentioned anything about not turning up for the dinner date. I was fuming and told him what I thought of him for not phoning to cancel the date. Yes, I was pissed off at being stood up! I knew at this point that Tarik was going to give me one of his diplomatic apology speeches which he did with a sad look on his face telling me that he'd been called away on business suddenly that evening and didn't have time to cancel the dinner date. He then went on repeating that he was sorry for all the inconvenience that he'd caused us all. Then suggested that he'd make up for it by taking the group sightseeing as there were a lot of interesting places to visit and see in Turkey which could be got to easily by car from Ankara for a day trip with lunch included.

Now remember the saying 'curiosity killed the cat'! Tarik did have a charming and charismatic personality when he needed to use it which could be turned on and off at a moment's notice. Possibly that's what drew me to him like a moth being drawn to a flame. I was attracted by his intelligence and knowledge of most topics which made him interesting company and not the usual type of rich bore normally encountered in night clubs. After I'd spoken to Tarik I asked my dancers if they would like to go sightseeing on our day off from the club. A couple of days later, Tarik phoned to ask how many people wanted to go on the trip. I told him that I'd spoken to the dancers and only three people were interested in going plus myself. His response was that two cars would be ample for the trip as some of his friends were coming too. The trip was planned for the following Sunday and took place.

The consequences of that day trip produced many strange effects on my body and life over the next few weeks with me clueless as to what was happening to both. I was gradually becoming used and demonized then my life dissolved rapidly into turmoil.

That's how it all began when I heard voices for the first time in my hotel room. Now I know that what I heard was coming from a stronghold of demons who were waiting and planning to enter my body. When it happened I became a hostage and a host for them to play their mind games and brainwashing with. After that fatal night when Tarik came into the club, nothing was ever quite the same for me again.

Chapter 4

Trip to Zelve

Today was Sunday and the day of the trip to Cappadocia that I was looking forward to. It's a highly recommended place for visitors to see in Turkey. I was pleased to have the chance to see it while I was working in Ankara and the Graeme Open Air Museum. I felt quite excited about the trip as I pulled up the blinds of my room and bright rays of sunlight filtered in. The weather outside looked good with a clear blue sky and promising for the trip. My alarm clock went off suddenly as I stood gazing out of the window. It was time to go and have my shower and get dressed quickly.

As I opened the door of my room I saw the girls were already dressed and waiting to go down for breakfast sitting on a couch in the corridor of the floor I lived on. We all went downstairs together and after breakfast went to sit in the lounge of the hotel to wait for the cars to arrive for the trip. The hotel lounge had large windows that gave a good view of anyone arriving at the hotel. I glanced at the clock in the lounge. It was nearly 10 am and I began to wonder if Tarik was going to turn up or not. At that moment the hands of the clock touched 10 am, the time we'd arranged to be picked up at the hotel. I stared at the clock and began to feel agitated. I had my doubts about agreeing to go on the trip and wished I had said no.

Suddenly, a black Mercedes Benz came into sight with another car following close behind. I guessed it was Tarik's with his friends. Both cars gradually came to a halt in front of the hotel. Tarik got out of his car and strolled into the lounge where we were waiting. He looked confident that morning and pleased with himself for being there He was wearing one of his polite smiles as he wished us all good morning. This gave me a false impression that he was in a good mood that day and determined it was going to be a success. He asked if we'd had breakfast. I replied that we had and noticed his sigh of relief when he said "let's go!" He then directed us all to the two waiting cars that were parked in front of the hotel. We arranged ourselves between the two cars and settled ourselves in for the journey that lay ahead. When Tarik got in the car he didn't say anything to me but slammed the door shut.

At that point I noticed his sudden change of mood as he settled himself into the driver's seat and put the key into the ignition. The sound that came out of that car was like all hell was being let loose. Looking back on that day now, it did seem strange from the moment the car doors were shut. From then on, a weird atmosphere appeared once we'd left Ankara behind in the distance with sudden eerie silences that kept occurring throughout the whole journey to Cappadocia. Here it comes! We never ended up seeing Cappadocia through the bad weather but went to Zelve instead. Taking my mind back to that Sunday morning so long ago, the weather that day was warm and sunny when we left the hotel but gradually as we left Ankara behind in the distance it began to change.

The blue sky disappeared and was replaced by a greyer one with heavy dark clouds. They looked foreboding as they formed above us as we drove on. The sky grew darker as we drove down endless winding roads and lanes. All of a sudden a strange silence engulfed the car that was quite eerie. At first I thought the silence could be due to very little traffic on the roads being a Sunday. This silence was different and strange. Nobody spoke and it was like everybody was being controlled by some unknown force whose power transformed the atmosphere each time it took place. It was unexplainable as everything in the car appeared to be normal but when this silence filled the car everyone seemed to become catatonic. When Tarik turned the car radio on it cut through the silence like a knife and changed the atmosphere back to normal. Then everyone in the car began to talk at the same time and this continued throughout the rest of the journey.

I'll never forget those sudden changes of atmosphere that kept taking place throughout that day. It was eerie and seemed to linger around us everywhere we went during that day. I also felt I was being watched by an invisible force that couldn't be seen but it could see us. I suddenly shivered and felt ice cold with fear and as if we were all being looked at by alien eyes on that stormy day as we drove on towards Cappadocia.

The atmosphere gradually changed and grew into an oppressive and heavy one during that journey. There were some unpredictable undertones that something evil was with us and waiting for the right moment to capture a victim in its clutches of dark energy. I felt uneasy and sensed a strange unknown force hovering around us once we'd left Ankara behind. The reason I could feel and sense these things was because I had the ability to do this being a sensitive and medium. I never knew this fact when these paranormal encounters began to surface on that trip.

Back in the car with the radio playing along with the hum of conversation from the people in my car, it was pleasant enough as we continued on towards Cappadocia. Dark clouds were now beginning to form in front of our car with a mist as the first light drops of rain began to fall onto the car. There was a swish as the windscreen wipers were turned on as the rain got heavier and beat down onto the roof of the car with a loud pounding sound. The sky was fearful and dark now as both cars got swept along into the gathering storm. With the radio playing Endless Love again in the background, we sped on with the wind howling around the car towards our destination with the rain pounding against the windows of the car. Suddenly, Tarik brought the car to a halt with a loud screeching sound and announced that were changing direction and going to Zelve instead of Cappadocia, as it was closer and we'd miss the worst part of the storm by going there instead.

He turned the car around and we changed direction and gradually picked up speed and drove on until we reached a signpost with Zelve City written on it. Tarik made another statement that "it's still going to take another hour before we reach there." After hearing this news I asked him if we could stop for a short break as everyone needed a warm drink including myself and urgently wanted to use the loo as we'd been travelling for some time. My remark seemed to have fallen on deaf ears so I mentioned we needed to stop a few times more. I guess he must have heard me as suddenly he pulled over at a signpost which had written on it 'Coffee Bar with Toilets'. Now the heavens opened up and rain poured down drenching us all as we got out of the cars. Everyone jumped out and rushed straight off to use the toilets then onto the cafeteria for drinks. When we'd done this we returned to the two waiting cars and continued onto Zelve. Now the daylight seemed to be fading.

The sky grew darker as the impending storm gathered and made it's descent upon the road we were now on. The force of the wind was now carrying us along down more twisting turbulent roads until the car came to another Halt. We were in front of a panorama of mud mounds that loomed up against a background of dark rocky hills that surrounded and covered the horizon. Tarik announced "we're here! This is Zelve." I thought "oh shit" as I got out of the car and wished I'd stayed in the hotel in Ankara for my day off. While contemplating these thoughts, there was a loud bang then lightning lit up the sky, followed by another thunderous bang from a short distance away.

We all had to make a dash towards the entrance of the caves getting soaking wet to achieve the task of buying tickets to see the caves. After we purchased the tickets, the next obstacle was to get to the caves. The entrance was up another steep hill of unlevelled ground to reach the entrance of the first cave. For once I thought I'd done the right thing wearing jeans and sensible shoes. By the time we reached the entrance to the cave, my feet were soaking wet as the rain hadn't stopped pouring down the entire day, oh what fun! Now I really looked like a drowned rat with my wet hair clinging to my face and a red nose. My clothes were soaking wet and clinging to my body and my feet were wet. Now I felt totally pissed off for coming on the trip as we reached the entrance to the cave. The daylight was cut off as we went in and we were in semi darkness apart from the lights that were placed around the walls of the caves.

It was necessary to pay attention not to lose one's balance and slip as it was quite a drop to the bottom of the cave. In the semi darkness of the cave, the walls looked mysterious with the matchstick-like figures that were carved onto them. All the figures were realistically painted and seemed to hold an air of great sorrow and pain in the way they'd been carved and painted with stories from the past that possibly had taken place in this area. Tarik took charge and acted as our guide and started explaining what the drawings on the walls were meant to represent and he told us a bit about the history of Zelve. I'd missed the first part of his guided tour and what he said but he caught my attention when he started talking about the Christians who might have suffered there.

He then explained what some of the individual carvings represented and the stories behind them. While Tarik was talking a strange cold chill passed over me as I gazed up at the matchstick-like figures. Some of the figures were hanging upside down being crucified, others were being tortured in different ways. I often wonder now if those tortured figures were in any way an omen of what lay ahead for me. Maybe I was being given a sign on that day? Shortly after that trip my life began to change drastically into one of nightmares and sleepless nights as I began to live a daily paranormal existence.

As I look back now thirty years later it had started out like any other day trip to get a break from my everyday problems and relax away from my job. The somewhat morbid atmosphere of the caves seemed to put a damper on the day adding to what we'd already experienced in the car with the eerie silences and the feeling of being watched on the journey. After the caves, all I wanted to do was have a nice cup of tea and a sit down. There was nowhere in sight to do this so we continued on seeing everything else at the museum. Everyone now seemed tired as the place had an oppressive negative energy that seemed to drain us. I thought what I felt was due to my vivid imagination and tried to dismiss it as I was determined to enjoy the rest of the day even though I was completely wet from head to toe. What we all needed was a warm drink and somewhere to sit down for a while. I couldn't put the blame on Tarik for the lousy day as we'd all agreed to come on the trip. It was nobody's fault that the weather was bad.

Due to the heavy downpour of rain there were quite a few mud slides that day. When we had finished sightseeing, we took a short cut to get to the car park down a steep hill and the ground was wet and slippery. By then I was really very tired and wasn't paying attention to where I was walking. I lost my balance and footing and fell and was about to go over the edge of the hill. Tarik reacted quickly and caught hold of me which stopped me from having a bad accident and rolling over the edge. Once he grabbed hold of me he didn't let me go for some time until I was ok. When I thanked him he didn't seem to hear but just kept holding onto me until we reached the car. Then he opened the door and put me onto the seat at the front. I sat in the car still a bit shaky waiting while Tarik went off to find the others.

Although I was safe and in the car now and should have felt better, I didn't. I felt deathly cold and lifeless like my energy had been drained out of my body. I couldn't tell the others about the unknown force of evil that I felt on that day which seemed to hover around me and our group in Zelve. My clothes were damp and I shivered not only from the cold but also from an unknown fear that seemed to cling to me. My heart pounded inside my chest and ears. Then suddenly Tarik opened the car door on the driver's side and got in quickly slamming the door shut. I could see he was wet, tired and nervous and couldn't wait to get away from that place as quickly as possible. Perhaps the strange atmosphere that I experienced was connected to the spirits of people who had possibly been tortured and died there. Deceased people's spirits can linger on and remain in a place.

Mediumistic or sensitive people would possibly sense this atmosphere quickly if they visited the place as some earth bound spirits can remain in a place forever until they are removed or put to rest. I felt relieved when Tarik came back to the car with the rest of the people and now we could leave. He started the car and put the windscreen wipers on as the rain continued to beat furiously against the car windows with a blinding force.

As we drove away from Zelve the lightning flashed across the dark sky. Now the rain was heavier and making it impossible to see in front of us. As the storm intensified with the occasional roll of thunder in the distance. After about an hour of our journey back to Ankara, the uncanny silence began taking place again in the car until someone asked for the radio to be turned on. This time it's effect didn't do much to lift the morbid atmosphere. Shortly after that trip my endless nightmare began taking place. Had we been drawn to that place that might be haunted by spirits of the dead through their suffering? Were they already with us and that was the reason why everyone felt so drained of energy and unusually tired? Had we picked some of the negative energy that lingered throughout that place?

Life is an unpredictable journey with many twists and turns taking place throughout our lives. Who really holds the answer why my nightmare took place? The journey back to Ankara took several hours and we stopped half way for lunch at a road-side restaurant as everyone seemed tired from the trip. There was very little conversation over lunch as everybody seemed to want to get back to Ankara as quickly as they could. The endless question that kept being asked throughout the rest of the journey was ''how much longer will it take?'' I felt the same as the others and just wanted to be back in my hotel. We arrived back in Ankara late afternoon and said our goodbyes to everyone and then Tarik finally dropped us off at our hotel.

That was the last I saw him apart from an odd day when he had a couple of hours to spare and he took me for tea to a typical Turkish tea house which lasted about an hour He then dropped me back to my hotel. Tarik did come into the club a couple times to see the show but left before the end. He phoned a couple of times to see how things were going with us at the club. Over the next couple of weeks everything drifted back into a normal daily routine for myself and the girls at the club.

Chapter 5

Strange Incidents Start Happening

It was a couple of weeks after the trip to Zelve that strange things began happening. One that I'll never forget took place after I'd phoned my husband in England. When we finished our call I placed the phone back on the receiver. After doing this I could still hear voices talking quite clearly. Thinking something was wrong with the phone, I called down to the receptionist of the hotel and told him about the interference caused by the faint voices. I told him it could be a crossed line causing the trouble on the phone. The receptionist came up to my room and checked the phone and line. After doing this he told me there was nothing wrong with either of the connections to my room as far as he could see. I remained puzzled and still thought it must have been a crossed line which I heard.

After talking to the receptionist I sat down on the bed still thinking about what had just taken place. Wishing that I was back home in England with my family instead of working in Ankara. The phone was on the bedside cabinet with my alarm clock and a small photo of my son. As I looked at my son's photo I did miss him and my husband. I was away from home and family, working with the show. I shivered and suddenly felt cold although it was a warm day outside. At that point the room seemed to become completely silent. Then out of nowhere a light rattling sound began quite close to me. I looked up and saw my son's photo on the bedside cabinet moving slightly. As I watched the photo it started to shake rapidly making a sharp beating sound on the cabinet. I just stared at the strange phenomenon and found it hard to believe but it was taking place in front of me and I was dumbfounded and terrified.

The first thoughts that came into my mind were that something bad had happened to my son or husband. Had there been an accident? I couldn't stop worrying as negative thoughts kept coming into my mind so I thought I'd call my husband again in England. I did this and spoke to him and asked if they were both alright. My husband said they were both fine and there was nothing to worry about. He also asked me why I'd called again that day. I didn't tell him the reason or about what had just taken place. My husband then told me to stop worrying so much and we said our goodbyes. I replaced the phone back onto the receiver and the call ended.

This was an example right at the beginning of the demonization showing how the voices can interfere with a person's life. The phone incident was the just the start of the terrible things that would come in a multitude of ways to confuse and turn my life upside down. Every night when I returned to the hotel after work in the early hours of the morning. At that time the hotel lay silent and still. One night when I was getting ready for bed and having a cup of tea, I heard a faint voice again and it puzzled me. This time I went down the corridor of the floor that I lived on to listen outside the various rooms that were close to mine to see if a radio or cassette was being played. There wasn't a sound coming from any of the other rooms near mine, they were all quiet. I went back to my room with no answer as to where the voices were coming from.

A few days later when I went to bed after returning from work, I was woken up suddenly with a jolt for no reason after only having slept for a very brief period. These type of disturbances were becoming consistent since the voices had arrived. My usual sleep pattern disappeared over the following days completely. Now the brief periods of sleep that I got were full of weird dreams and night terrors which I'd never experienced before.

My room in the hotel was situated on the second floor that faced the street so I could hear all the sounds of the traffic. On this particular morning the noise of this car I heard would have risen the dead with its loud screeching sound filling my room when it revved up outside my hotel window. The noise was unbearably loud as the car's engine was started. It was like all hell was being let loose with fury. The smell of burnt rubber came into my room from the tires as the car took off down the road with a devil sitting in the driver's seat. Defiantly on a journey heading for suicide at an infernal speed.

I attempted to sleep again and did so for about an hour. Then was woken up again this time with a sharp pain in my arm like after having an injection. I heard a voice and it said ''Janna.'' It sounded like Tarik. Now I was really feeling nervous and agitated through all the disturbances and not being able to sleep with all this shit going on. A thought crossed my mind. Was it Tarik going nuts? He'd mentioned to me that he didn't sleep well because of noises in his head since his accident. Was I picking up a form of telepathic communication from him? Was he having treatment in hospital for his condition?

I'd advised him to see a doctor and get some help for the condition. When I thought I'd heard Tarik's voice this appeared logical after the conversations I'd had with him. That's why I thought it might be telepathic communication as I'd recently seen a program   about it from America on TV. He also mentioned that after the accident he had seen a doctor who thought his condition with noises was nothing to worry about.

Over the years I've read quite a bit about what people do to get rid of noises in the ears or head. They try alcohol to help lessen their problem. It won't help. It will remain and plague the victim even more. More alcohol will never resolve anything but create an alcoholic over time. You might think I'm nuts! I believe noises left behind after any traumatic issue can be used by a demon to create yet another vice. No-one will ever look into this situation or suspect it's being caused by a demon. That's my belief.

In Ankara I was confronted head on by the powers of darkness during the days with the voices who were misleading me from the first time that I heard them. Probably it wasn't Tarik that I heard but I continued thinking what I was hearing was telepathy being sent to me by Tarik. It wasn't Tarik but unclean spirits who were entering my body and mind as the demonization took place with me being unaware of what was happening to me.

I'd never experienced anything with voices before the phone incident or previously when I'd known Tarik in Izmir a few years earlier. There had never been any sort of attachment to him previously with voices. Over the following weeks the voices became a permanent fixture in my life and were disturbing me constantly day and night. Each time they started I did my best to ignore them but they were with me to stay. Every night when I returned to the hotel tired after working long hours at the club with my show and went to bed they'd be there to disturb my sleep. I couldn't escape this nightmare. It was now ongoing endlessly when I tried to sleep. I'd then wake up suddenly in the darkness of my room with the voices in my head.

I lay awake for hours in the darkness listening to voices finding it impossible to sleep. As I started to live with my endless hell state living with a condition that I couldn't stop! That's how this unknown phenomenon rooted itself in my life and body. Generally when these incidents were taking place a sudden chillness would fill the room I'd start to feel cold and shiver as the dark energy infiltrated my body. That's what started my ongoing traumatic stress which I've lived with since Ankara. And what's continued holding my life in its deadly bondage.

Once this network of demons came into my world I became their victim and host for them to reside in. When this was all happening in Ankara I hadn't a clue what was going on. I'd never experienced anything like this before and started dreading going back to the hotel each night after work. Now I was worried all the time about being alone in my room. I'd travelled and lived around the world in many different hotel rooms but this one was now haunting me. Over the passing days it became frightening to be alone.

Whenever I came into the room an eerie feeling swept over me and left me deathly cold each time. I kept questioning myself about these incidents and asking myself were they really happening to me or was it in my imagination. I'd never heard voices before and it puzzled me as to why now. What were these voices and where did they come from? They were there nightly and I could hear them. I was nervous and on edge and getting worried about how I was going to cope if they didn't stop.

At that time of night the hotel lay dormant and still apart from the occasional sound of the lift as it went between floors when it was being used by the staff of the hotel. The whole hotel was completely silent. What did these whispering voices want and why was this happening to me? Over the passing days it gradually became clearer to understand what they were saying. They brought with them a depressive distortion to my life with their spiritual warfare. Then my ongoing battle living between two worlds really began.

It was the beginning of summer and quite warm each night around 4.30am in the morning when I came in from work. After being in the room for a short time I started to notice the temperature would begin to drop and turn cold. Before this strange phenomenon took place my room had always been stuffy and I'd have to open the windows for fresh air. The difference was obvious now but I still tried to dismiss what was actually taking place as the atmosphere in my room continued to remain uncanny and eerie.

I didn't want to return to the hotel as the days passed by and I was nervous when I had to return after work. I started getting a rush of adrenalin each time I put the key in the lock of the door to open it. My heart would start pounding and beating loudly inside my chest and ears. I'd dread going to bed and sleeping because I knew they'd be there to torment me nightly. I looked at my small travelling clock on the bedside cabinet.

It was nearly 6 am in the morning and I was still awake. I needed to get some sleep. When I finally did the first rays of light were coming through the small cracks in the blinds of my room. They threw a strange translucent light across the room as I tossed and turned in bed trying to sleep. Then I started to shiver again as the room turned even colder. The dawn of a new day crept slowly into my room bringing with it a tidal wave of unknown fear that raced around at random in my mind and body.

I knew by then something sinister was being unleashed into my life which would change the whole course of my existence forever. At that time in Ankara I'd no idea of what was about to engulf me as my mind was working overtime with negative thoughts like a bombarding hurricane. The thoughts and fears swept over me and held me captive in that hotel room. While the demon gang unleashed their torments into my entire body with their nightly warfare. I attempted to block them and sleep but waves of fear swept over me. What was happening to me? I finally drifted off into another troubled disturbing sleep as the light of another dawn came into the room and another day began.

The whole condition had become permanent since the day trip to Zelve. Now I sensed an energy covering my entire body that had started to make me feel lethargic all the time. Was I being stalked and a victim of this unknown energy? I couldn't find an answer as to why my whole life was being attacked by the realms of darkness.

Was it to do with meeting Tarik again and the type of fatal attraction there was between us both? I feel that could have probably given the demons access and a chance to move in on this situation and make things materialize. Yes, it was a temptation that I knew I must face and resist as I'd done years before in Izmir. I knew nothing could ever develop with any relationship as I was already married and I'd never cheat on my husband as our marriage was a happy one. Meeting Tarik again was doomed to go nowhere. However, after meeting again on that fatal night when he came into the club, all sorts of strange supernatural things did start taking place on a daily basis.

Together with a vortex of evil that seemed to be closer with each passing day that was descending into my world. Ankara was like any other town when dusk fell upon its streets with invisible demons prowling and stalking in the darkness of night. If only I'd known what was about to unfold into my life but I'd no idea of the destruction that was about to strike me.

Danger lurked when the demonic spirits made their entrance with their demonization in my body. The effects of this condition are horrific and disastrous for any person who has them. I know because I've experienced them myself. I began to suffer with the first symptoms and signs that began taking place with pains in my entire body. From then on I was always feeling tired and lifeless and not my usual self. Then I recognized that something strange was taking place inside my body which was making me feel ill. I became a hostage of the nightly attacks that were causing a great deal of pain inside of my body. These attacks were being done by the perpetrators from hell inside my body. When this takes place in a person's body from that moment on life turns into an endless nightmare. The Serpent coils around the body and attempts to squeeze one's life away.

Then the worst tortures begin both mentally and physically in the whole body from the crown of the head to the soles of the feet. I'm telling you this from my own personal experience of living with this is a horrific ordeal daily for many years and from being terrorized by demons for half of my lifetime.

How would you feel living with continuing traumatic stress and nightmares throughout the day and night and having whispering voices coming from inside your own body? There is no escape from this prison of torments waiting to attack every part of the body. I'm telling you that it is a hellish condition living with permanent squatters from hell inside you. It's horrific! Do you want to know more? I've been living with this condition 24 hours a day for over thirty years. Demons, devils or unclean spirits are all equivalent to having parasites in your body. That is what they are.

Demons are a form of energy without a body but don't worry they'll be using yours to experience feeling human and take over your life if they can. They came to murder, destroy and ruin a person's life, nothing else. They find a victim and use them as a host to reside in. That's it in a few words and that's what they want! You can imagine how my health is now as I've waited for well over thirty years for my deliverance.

Chapter 6

Voices and Phenomena

Looking back on Ankara now I wished I'd recognized earlier where my trouble was coming from. So I could have stopped a lot of heartache that the issue brought into my family life and career. If I could turn back the clock in time and change what took place, I would. Without any understanding of what was going on I even thought it could be God speaking to me. It wasn't! The evil spirits were using God as a tactic to get to me. I learnt the hard way through my ongoing battles with the demonic gangs that they were trying to manipulate my body and life.

When I was in Ankara I explained my condition in a letter by saying it was like being tuned constantly into a radio station that you couldn't turn off. This describes exactly what the condition feels like once it's attached to you. It's a frightening experience to be living with especially having voices inside your mind and body constantly which are tuned into whatever you are doing. I thought it was telepathic communication for quite a while. It's like a connection between two people receiving information from each other where both parties are receptive.

Over time as my condition developed! The voices became more abusive saying a variety of horrific things which worried and shocked me. My next thought was that voices were coming from demonic spirit people who might want to talk with me. I kept hoping that the whole condition would go away but it didn't. Then I began to get sensations of being stabbed many times. While the demons were doing this they'd be whispering abusive things about the Catholic Church saying that I was going to suffer in a similar ways to Christ. At that point I began to experience pains throughout my body.

A few days later I began having teeth problems. I did the logical thing and booked myself into the dentist. This ended with a horrific ordeal. He examined my teeth and couldn't see where the trouble was coming from to begin with. Then he found a couple of teeth that could be causing the trouble and he advised me to have them taken out. Here it come's! I ended up spending seven hours in the dentist's chair and I became very ill. I actually collapsed several times. However, the teeth were finally taken out. The dentist informed me that he'd never seen or had such a difficult case extracting teeth. All my teeth had many roots and he'd never come across this before. It seems I was very 'unusual'.

After having my teeth taken out I was too ill to work that night. From then on I was continuously feeling ill with new pains developing in different areas of my body. This was unusual for me as I had been a fairly fit person before the voices came. Now I was worried. How was I going to cope if I was always feeling ill? Being a dancer and an all-round entertainer and managing a show takes a lot of energy. The ongoing stress with the condition was draining my vitality and life force away. During this period I continued working with the show but was finding it hard as I was continuously feeling tired and ill.

Another frightening incident occurred shortly after I'd had my teeth out. I'd gone to bed as usual around 6 am in the morning and slept for a very brief period. This time I was woken up gasping for air and being strangled! Alien hands were pressing tightly down around my throat trying to stop my breathing. I couldn't see the invisible assailant but it was attempting to choke me. I kept gasping trying to breathe as the attack grew worse. Then I made an attempt to shout for help but no sound came out of my throat. The intensity of the attack was terrifying. Who was doing this to me? I continued trying desperately to open my mouth and breathe. I made several attempts to scream but no sound came out!

The invisible assailant squeezed down harder on my throat to stop me breathing and strangle me. Now I was fighting for my life and frightened. At the time I didn't realize that the attack was coming from the inside of my body and being done to me by residents from hell who wanted to kill me. In my mind I cried out to God to help me! A few seconds later the morning prayers began from the mosque which was quite close to the hotel. The sound of the prayers echoed loudly across Ankara and into my room. As the prayers continued the pressure around my throat began to lessen and the choking feeling began to ease. My breathing gradually regained its normal state.

After this attack I lay in bed for some time in a shocked state unable to move. I can't forget that night and the fear it created. I was left terrified after that attack and in a very traumatic state. As the early morning light of another day began in Ankara, I was still asking myself the question who had been attacking me and what would they do next? Who'd believe me if I told anyone about the strange experiences that I was having?

It was only a few days previously that I'd sent a letter off to my husband regarding what I thought was the truth about my strange experiences. Would he believe me or think I was joking? That letter was the biggest mistake I ever made and helped to break up my long marriage which subsequently ended in divorce. The letter hammered the first nail of destruction into my marriage. I also believe it caused the beginning of my husband's heart condition through the stress and misunderstandings that it brought into our marriage. Demonic strongholds are the biggest perpetrators of destruction in people's lives.

I did approach the Church for advice to see if they could help me with my experiences. I needed them to give me some practical spiritual help to end my nightmare so I could get my life back on track. After initially seeing a priest in Ankara, the next step I took was to visit a doctor to get some medication to help me sleep. I thought that the medication might calm things down and I'd feel better. I took the medicine but it didn't stop the nightly terrors which continued on while I was working with the show. I did my best to hide what was happening to me as I didn't want to lose the contract with the club and my job. During that time the strange phenomena continued haunting my body and life.

I was reaching breaking point when one more problem arrived. The club manager asked me to do a free show for a General who'd be visiting Ankara in a few days. The manager informed me that the club was obligated to do this show and so was I. There had already been an official request to do the show for that occasion. From my past experience of working with dancers, I knew they didn't like doing free shows and neither did I but this one would have to be done.

That evening after our show I called the dancers together and explained the situation about the free show we had to do. We'd no choice in the matter. There was a commotion but eventually the dancers agreed to do the show. Well, we did it and it was a great success with the military audience at the stadium. It was packed with soldiers being a military occasion and with the visit of the

General to Ankara. The show was successful and the dancers enjoyed the applause and ovation from the audience. I saluted the photo of Ataturk and the stadium erupted with applause, shouts and stamping. Then the General stood up and saluted the men and myself to more applause. So in the end everything turned out ok and we received little 'thank you' gifts and an afternoon tea.

Around that time I was expecting a replacement dancer to arrive from England to join my show who'd would become the head girl so I could return to England for a short break to sort out my private life. About a week later a friend of Tarik's came into the Club and I told him to let Tarik know that the 'sports stuff' he wanted would be arriving soon with someone who was coming out from England to join my show.

A few minutes after I'd spoken to him a kind of rattling sound began. Then the chain with a cross I was wearing broke and another tooth cracked. It was all very strange and frightening. Now it was becoming clearer that something sinister was going on. The things I had been experiencing were not happening in my imagination! Had someone put a curse on me and that's why these terrible things were taking place non-stop? That same evening shortly after those two incidents, Tarik strolled into the club to see the show and asked me to join him after work for a coffee in the bar close to the hotel.

After the two incidents I was desperate to talk to someone about my experiences since the trip to Zelve. That's why I agreed to meet him in the bar near the hotel hoping to discuss my problems with him. I wanted to find out if he knew anyone in Ankara who could help me. Not realizing that the meeting Tarik after work that night was going to have lasting effects upon my life.

Chapter 7

The Meeting and Consequences

I never knew at this point that I was heading for more upheaval in my life by meeting Tarik at the bar. It would result in a chain effect over the coming weeks which would involve explaining my actions to my husband about that night. After I'd agreed to meet Tarik, I returned to the hotel after work with the dancers and got changed. Then I took a walk to the café which was close to our hotel. I mentioned to one of the dancers before leaving the hotel that I wouldn't be long. I was just going to have something to eat with Tarik and was then coming back. I'd no idea at the time what the outcome of that meeting was going to bring. Looking back now on arranging to meet Tarik on my own after work wasn't normally done. Usually the whole the group were invited together for a snack.

On that fateful night I felt driven to find an answer to the problem that I was now suffering with twenty four hours a day. The whole issue was inexplicable and paranormal. It had worried me from the first time when I heard the voices. Since then it had affected my health and my life had deteriorated at a rapid pace with disastrous effects. Here it comes! The consequences of that night and seeing Tarik ended up affecting the rest of my life forever. If I hadn't been suffering with being demonized I would never have agreed to meet him.

I needed someone to confide in and Tarik seemed to be the ideal person to talk to. He knew so many people and possibly someone might be able to help me. When I arrived at the café Tarik was already there waiting and told me that he had some business to tie up at his place first, then he'd fix us something to eat and we could talk. From the moment he said 'my place' I began to feel uneasy about the situation that I'd got myself into and went into panic mode.

By the time we reached his car I could hear his voice rambling on about the business he had to get done which was so important to him. He patted my hand saying that he'd have time listen to what I wanted to tell him when he'd finished what he had to do. Once in the car I tried to concentrate on what he was saying, growing more tense and nervous by the minute and trying to remain calm. I should have foreseen what the situation could develop into. My mind kept ticking over non-stop repeating to me…''Why did you accept to go to his place?'' I could see clearly then that it could turn into a compromising situation that I'd have to deal with.

These words kept turning over in my head warning me about what I'd got into. I'd given my dancers this message so many times about being careful of accepting invitations to apartments. Now I was in car with Tarik doing it myself. Suddenly the atmosphere in the car seemed to become very warm and I began to sweat which I rarely do. My nervous system took over and I began to feel sick thinking about what the outcome might be.

The strange phenomenon that I was experiencing was blinding my judgement. I was desperate to talk with someone about the predicament that I was in with the damn voices which were beginning to drive me nuts. I was vulnerable and had made a rash move without thinking what my actions might bring looking for a bloody answer to get rid of the damn voices that wouldn't stop. Living with the condition was becoming too stressful for me to cope with alone. I needed help. I was desperate to find a solution to end what was happening to me. I felt frantic with worry and didn't predict the repercussions that the meeting would bring. My stomach began to churn and I felt sick by the time we reached Tarik's apartment. He gave me something to drink then went off to attend to some business on the phone which went on for nearly an hour. When that ended I thought I'd be able to talk to him about what I had been suffering with since my time in Zelve.

I didn't get round to telling him anything about what was worrying me as the whole situation gradually became compromising and got out of hand. Tarik started making advances thinking that I'd gone to his apartment to have sex with him which I hadn't. I'd gone for a different reason. I'll say one thing... he tried it on but didn't lose control of himself completely which I respect. He did however have a bit of a 'turn' and said that he wasn't going to take me back to my hotel and that I was going to have to stay with him until the morning. It was a case of lump it or like it. Then he ignored me and went to bed and advised me to do the same.

I couldn't take any more of the situation that I'd got myself into and told him that I was leaving for my hotel. He yelled that there were no taxis about at that time of the morning. I replied that I'd walk if I had to and left. Once I'd gone from his apartment I had to walk quite away until luckily I finally managed to find a taxi and got a ride back to my hotel. By the time I got back there I was a nervous wreck and extremely tired. When I went to reception to get my key I was told that there'd been a message left from my husband in England who'd called shortly after I'd left the hotel to meet Tarik.

It was unusual to get such messages as I generally spoke to my husband by phone during the daytime. Here comes the next bit of good news! One of my dancers took the call from my husband and told him that I'd gone to the café near the hotel with Tarik and would be back soon. When I was given the message it was early morning in England and my husband would be asleep. I decided I'd call him later that day, which I did. I felt tired and depressed about everything that had happened through meeting Tarik. It was all my fault and I felt very guilty about the whole episode.

Later that day I phoned my husband and explained to him what had taken place and of course he didn't believe me even though I was telling him the truth. I also mentioned what had been happening to me with the strange paranormal experiences. He must have thought it was an excuse to cover up what I'd been doing. It was yet another mistake. By telling him the truth, I'd taken the wrong action that night. It was going to break up my marriage. Telling the truth brought crucial changes to the chess board of my life. This game had already begun and would continue over many years. I was a pawn in this game being played now with the shield of truth.

I thought my husband knew my character well enough to know that I wouldn't lie to him. We'd been through a lot together over the years. Over the phoned he asked me to be truthful about what had taken place that night. After I'd explained in detail what took place and about the paranormal incidents, I knew from his reaction that my husband hadn't believed a word that I'd said. It only seemed to make things worse between us as he thought that I'd made up the story to hide what had actually taken place. He thought I was trying to cover up for not being in the hotel when he'd called from England. Knowing now that he didn't believe or trust me anymore disappointed me because I'd told him the truth. Now I understand more clearly what the voices could lead me into doing. They could bring more disastrous effects on my life's journey living with demons. Eventually my marriage did end with a divorce although we stayed together and remained friends until my husband's death and I never remarried.

A couple of wise saying's:

The damnedest thing in the world is doing the right thing for the wrong reason.

All the humor of the situation is lost in the reality of being a part of it.

I was told these wise words by an American real gentleman with a very funny sense of humor on the philosophy of life which was a tonic for me at that period of my life when laughter was such rare thing.

Chapter 8

Strange Weird Manifestations

Being extremely worried now I didn't know how long I could keep coping with my health deteriorating rapidly. Who'd believe my story if I told anyone about what I was suffering with? Finally I took the decision to confide in one of my dancers who came from Zambia by telling her about the voices and the trouble that I was having with sleeping at night. She didn't seem surprised at all and told me that in her country sometimes these sort of things happened to people. She then gave me some information about what she thought I might be hearing telling me a little bit about spirits or demons who attach themselves to people. Saying it might be what I was experiencing and that if it was, they must be taken away quickly. Then she suggested that I should try to see a priest or a person who deals with these types of conditions.

Aiming to cheer me up, she added that once the spirits were removed from me, the disturbances would stop. After being given this information I felt a lot calmer and decided to make an appointment to see a priest from the church that I attended on Sundays to get some help solving my problems. I made an appointment after mass that Sunday to see a priest and felt better after doing this. The following week I went to the appointment and saw the priest which didn't turn out to be very helpful or resolve anything.

It left me still facing my ordeal alone and stuck living with the voices of the demons until I could find a solution. I was desperate now not being able to sleep and didn't know what to do. I was responsible for being in charge of a show working abroad on a contract and it was all getting too much for me. After seeing the priest I went to visit a doctor who gave me some tablets to take which were supposed to calm everything down. They didn't do much good either. Many times I felt like I was on a roller coaster ride that I couldn't get off. The disturbances grew and so did my nervous and agitated state every night when I had to return to the hotel after work. I dreaded facing the situation that was draining me through being over-tired all the time. Now I only slept for brief periods and woke up suddenly hearing the voices. Sometimes they appeared to stop for a short period and when this happened I'd lie in bed feeling anxious for hours, finding it hard to go back to sleep. How can you sleep with an unknown assailant waiting in the darkness to begin attacking and tormenting you?

In the beginning I thought the voices could be a figment of my imagination playing tricks with me but now I know they were real as I've experienced their torments for well over thirty years. Being able to write my story is truly due to the grace of God. Nothing was ever the same again after Ankara. My life just turned into an ongoing horror story that I've been forced to live with ever since. I hope one day to be able to help others who are suffering with a similar situation so they're not alone with no one to confide in. Through my experience I've gained first-hand knowledge of what demonization is so I know that the condition exists and that it's a real one. Many people around the world are still suffering with it in silence.

Having previously phoned my husband to explain the circumstances in which I had found myself in Ankara after weeks of suffering with the condition, I also decided to write to my husband and explain truthfully what I thought was happening to me. In the letter to him I mentioned the strange incidents and sensations that I'd been having since the day trip to Zelve. Once again this was to result in a negative situation as far as my marriage was concerned.

One afternoon when the hotel was silent and still with none of the usual noises going on suddenly the silence was broken by a sharp knock on my door. I thought it might be one of my dancers coming to see me about something as they often did on their day off. I opened the door to be confronted by one of the waiters from the hotel holding a large carcass of a dead sheep still dripping with blood from recently being slaughtered.

He greeted me saying it had been killed for the Moslem holiday. The stench of the fresh blood filled the air and continued oozing out of the body of the dead sheep. Now blood was dripping onto the floor of my room. I wanted to scream and tell him to move that bloody thing away from me but I kept my cool and told him sharply to take it away. He replied saying he'd just bought the sheep to my room to show it to me. On that day of the religious holiday a sheep was always slaughtered and then eaten on that night.

I told him bluntly that I wasn't interested in seeing a dead sheep in my hotel bedroom and asked him to take it away straight away. At that moment he took some of the sheep's blood and smeared it onto my hotel room's door. Now he'd gone too far and I started to scream at him hysterically to get that sheep out of my sight and room! I couldn't stop screaming and told him that I was going to report him to the management of the hotel.

A few minutes later I went downstairs and complained to the management about the waiter and the incident that had just taken place. They appeared to have no knowledge of why the waiter had done this. They reassured me that they'd send one of their staff to clean up the blood from my room and door. The blood was cleaned off but I couldn't get the incident out of my mind as it struck me as being very strange. Why my door and no one else's? The bleeding sheep incident was just another one on the growing list of weird and uncanny events that went on endlessly.

Another day when I returned to the hotel after rehearsals I found that a large chair had been put in my room, which I never asked for or wanted. Whenever there was something confusing or troubling going on the voices would be there whispering and tormenting me as well. That's how demon gangs work to destroy you with their brainwashing process that goes on nonstop to drive you nuts. Next I thought Tarik had paid someone to do these terrible things to me. Looking back now he led a very busy life and I don't believe he would have bothered to do those type of things against me… it's ridiculous.

Then I felt God was involved in some way, knowing nothing about demonic warfare. My thoughts just kept turning from one thing to another and then onto was it black magic. Could someone be instigated a form of that against me because I was Christian. I then thought that God might be testing me in some way. How foolish of me God wouldn't do such tormenting things to people. Being totally ignorant of how the devil works to ensnare a victim and gain a host. No I didn't recognize the devils at work, stupid me! I know I might sound dumb but I'd never heard about people being attacked in this way.

I continued praying to God for an answer of why these things were happening to me, but nothing stopped. The alien voices that I kept hearing just continued brainwashing me with ongoing rubbish. With me not having a clue of what was really going on. Then at one stage I thought that God might be talking to me. Stupid isn't it! I was ignorant and the network of demons took advantage of the situation.

For anyone who's having this type of traumatic condition you'll get no mercy from any demon gang who invade a human body. Demons are just there to apply every evil torment and cruelty with sadism that they can inflict on their victim. Their aim is to use a body and abuse it while it's their host. Then they'll drag a victim down into the realms of despair onto the threshold of death's door if they can. They'll then continue tormenting you, until they hope you've had enough suffering and want to die. Things in Ankara gradually developed into a highly traumatic state while I waited for a replacement dancer to arrive from England. She was bringing some items that Tarik needed which he'd asked me to get him. I gave him the items one afternoon at the hotel after the dancer arrived from England and that was the last time I saw him.

I worked in Ankara throughout July then left for Istanbul with my show. On the day we were leaving the girls spent time saying their usual goodbyes to the boyfriends they'd made while we were in Ankara. Eventually the taxis arrived at the hotel for us to leave. Then we started loading our mountain of luggage into the taxis and a van. After all that we headed for the coach station to catch the coach for Istanbul. The weather that day was dreary with clouds and a light mist covering the skyline of Ankara as we left the place behind in the distance. Being an optimist by nature, I kept hoping that the various strange incidents would stop once I'd left Ankara behind along with all the supernatural activities and manifestations.

I was desperate and hoping that by moving on with the show we'd get a fresh start in Istanbul. This would give me a chance to sort my life out as it was in a mess. There was a changed in the weather and it got brighter as we got closer to Istanbul with rays of sunlight bathing the coach. By the time we reached the coach station it had turned into a lovely day with a cloudless sky. I didn't realize that it wasn't going to be the end of my story but just the beginning of things to come. Istanbul was going to end up being a short stay for my show.

On our arrival in Istanbul, Mr. Macy was there as usual waiting for us. He ushered us into taxis and took us straight to the hotel where we'd be staying within walking distance from his office. He found us a decent hotel that was central and this was a priority to keep the peace with the dancers. Also it wasn't too far from the club where they'd be working.

I hoped to get things sorted out quickly with the show and then leave for England. The next day I met the boss at the club and made the arrangements for the show to start quickly at the club. While I was in Istanbul I had to fix rehearsal times to make sure the routines were presentable for the opening night. The new dancer who'd become head girl needed to feel confident in handling everything to do with the show as well before I left. Everything ran smoothly and I completed all the rehearsals within a few days and the opening night with the show went ok and the club was pleased.

Now it was time for me to leave for England to get my own problems sorted out with my husband. My health at this time wasn't good plus I was worrying a lot about the problems with my marriage which were occupying my mind non-stop. Would my marriage be strong enough to weather the storm or not? Would I lose all I held dear in my life because of the strange experiences? I kept hoping things would change and get better to end my ongoing nightmare.

Chapter 9

My Return to England

At last I was going home to England and leaving the horrors of Ankara behind me that were drawing me into a strange unreal paranormal world of deception and lies. I was about to board my flight for my journey home to England feeling tense and uneasy about what lay ahead for me. My husband's image kept looming up in front of me. I'd already explained everything to him about the night when I wasn't in the hotel in Ankara when he called from England. I just couldn't stop worrying about what would be the outcome of that conversation when I got home. From the time I boarded the flight, my stomach didn't stop churning up through nervous tension and this lasted throughout the flight back to England.

The journey was nearly over now and we were about to arrive and touch down on the tarmac of Heathrow Airport. I was now feeling terribly nervous anticipating seeing my husband. I picked up my hand luggage and left the plane with the rest of the passengers from my flight. And followed them down to the baggage hall to get my case and then onwards to the customs area for the usual baggage check. My heart was pounding loudly now in my chest and ears. As I walked with the rest of the passengers towards the door that lead into the arrivals area where I knew my husband would be waiting for me.

At this point I began to feel faint and I broke into a hot sweat that began to cover my entire body. I walked through the doors into the arrivals area where people were waiting for the incoming passengers off the flights. Now I was feeling even more fearful at the prospect of seeing my husband. Entering the arrivals area I spotted my husband in the crowd and waved to him. He walked over to me but said nothing as he helped me with my luggage. We then walked out of the airport building together in silence and headed for the parking area of the airport where my husband's car was parked.

When we reached the car he opened the door for me to get in. I hesitated and waited for him to say something to break the silence. Nothing happened and he remained silent while putting my luggage into the boot. I then made another attempt to talk to him again as we got into the car but there was still no response. My husband started the car and we began our journey home without saying a word. I'll never forget the atmosphere in the car that day. It was sad and very strange for both of us not to be talking. Usually my husband wanted to hear all the news about the show and the gossip about everything that had occurred where I'd been working. This journey home held the weird strange silence that I'd experienced before on that day trip to Zelve. After my arrival home, the next few weeks were filled with more unexpected supernatural incidents. They began taking place non-stop and helped to ruin my family life.

The premonition that I'd had in Turkey was now in motion and becoming my reality. Nothing would ever be the same again for us as a family. I understood this fact clearly in the car on that journey home from the airport. The damage had already been done to my marriage. I knew that my husband was never going to trust or believe me when I told him about what I'd been suffering with in Ankara. When we finally arrived home I was happy to see my son but even he seemed to be somewhat distant from me. I guess it was normal as he was young at the time and didn't know what was going on between his parents. He may also have been wondering why I'd come back early and alone without the rest of the dancers. The whole situation must have appeared strange to him seeing his parents acting so distant towards each other.

I understood how my husband felt emotionally thinking that I'd had an affair with Tarik and cheated on him. Since I'd taken my marriage vows with him I'd never broken them with anyone else. I couldn't do that because I respected my husband. The situation that I'd got myself into with Tarik in Ankara was mainly due to what I was suffering with at that time. He was a temptation that I turned away from due to being married. Now back in England, I repeated to my husband the truth about everything that had taken place on that night. He still didn't believe me. That evening after dinner when we were alone and my son had gone to bed, I had told my husband what I thought was happening to me truthfully still not realizing that I was being demonized by spirits who were already inside my body.

After our conversation the atmosphere at home continued to be tense. The condition from Turkey constantly bothered me over many days. And I couldn't believe what was still happening to me. The voices and supernatural experiences I talked to my husband about made no logical sense to him. Being demonized assassinated our relationship and gradually it became unbearable for us both. My husband simply didn't believe what I claimed was happening to me making me feel ill and confused.

We'd been married for around twenty four years with a reasonably happy relationship. It's not to say that we didn't have up's and downs during those years, we did. However, previously we'd always managed to sort out all the difficulties that confronted us but this time we couldn't. What was happening to me wasn't an ordinary situation but a paranormal one.

After being home for about a week, terrible pricking sensations and pains in my head began. I thought someone might be attacking me with voodoo and using a doll to do this as I'd heard about this magic. Over the passing weeks my health issues got worse and my husband couldn't understand what was wrong with me. He started saying there was something mentally wrong with me. All I wanted to do was get well and return to work as we needed money quickly to pay our bills at home. That didn't happen right away. The strange condition just clung onto my body and mind I couldn't get rid of it.

Being at home now I dwelt on my situation daily as it became more unbearable to live with. I still didn't grasp what my condition really was that was causing me so much stress and worry. What was happening to my whole life and health? Doing my best to settle into my everyday life at home, I looked for a job and managed to find a part time one that would help keep a little money coming in weekly until I felt well enough to go back to work with another show.

I'd been advised by a priest that I'd seen in Istanbul to get confirmed as quickly as I could. He'd explained to me that by doing this it would help me with what I was suffering with. By bringing me closer to God, healing would gradually begin to take place. From then on I made every effort to attend church more and hoped by doing this that things would get better. I contacted a priest whose name I'd been given and went to see him. I told him briefly my story. He also advised me to be confirmed and gave me all the information that I needed to go ahead and do this. Over the following months I attended several teaching study days until I was finally confirmed into the church in September 1983. However, after being confirmed my suffering and torments didn't stop but continued.

Soon after being confirmed, someone that I knew mentioned to me about some 'healers' who might be able to help me. This started me on another journey of seeing healers and having hands-on sessions a couple of times a week. These sessions did gradually seem to have some effect and help ease the condition down somewhat. All healing comes from God and is channeled through the healers to the patient. That's basically what I believe. All I can say is that it did help me.

I've often wondered over the years why this frightful endless ordeal came into my life. No doubt many people who suffer with long term illness must ask that same question. About five months passed by enduring night terrors and pain but then there seemed to be an improvement taking place in my health following quite a few healing sessions. This made me think that my nightmare was coming to an end as I began to feel my old self again.

During this time we were gradually becoming very short of money since there were no shows taking place throughout that period. The dancers had finished their contracts a couple of months previously and come home. We had bills coming in non-stop as usual and needed money desperately. My part time job paid very little as I was only working a few days a week so there wasn't enough money for our general living expenses.

My health at that time appeared somewhat better but I was still hearing the voices and being brainwashed with horrendous stories about my husband. Suggesting that he was gay and warning me to be careful about leaving my son with him. Why I believed this rubbish that was being put into my mind by the demon gang I don't know. Having voices going on in your head non-stop when being demonized is a horrific ordeal in itself. It creates ongoing havoc that muddles ones thoughts making it hard to analyze what's the truth. I was being bombarded daily with this type of spiritual warfare which is still going on to a certain degree today. The difference now is that I know what I'm dealing with but at the beginning of my demonization I was ignorant of what the demons were up to.   When my mind was being bombarded with different types of corruptions to provoke fear into my mind with the voices with treats of what they could do to me.

Thoughts of this nature were being planted into my mind about Tarik suggesting that he was involved and doing these attacks as a form of revenge. He was the main candidate in line for the devils to use, then my husband.

Despite the terrible suffering with daily pricking sensations in my head, chest pains and aching all over my body, I never stopped battling on to get well. This condition imprisoned my body and life since it began. It's a macabre ordeal to live and survive with in one's daily life.

Back to my story… I took the decision to try and work again and started auditioning for dancers to make another group. After a couple of months I managed to do this. I was given a six month contract to work in Italy and then go onwards to Greece. I managed to keep working throughout that period although I was still suffering.

Due to my condition, I had to take a lot of breaks from show business. During those periods I did a lot of in-store promotion work to survive and pay the bills. After quite a break from show business I eventually decided to give it another try and started auditioning for dancers again. Eventually I found four girl dancers and two girl singers and started rehearsals. In this show I had two backing singers to work with me and the four dancers as it was a variety show. Rehearsals began and went ok for the first few weeks although I still wasn't feeling well. I managed to cover up the fact at rehearsals most days. I was still hoping that my condition would disappear gradually once I started work and got my life back on track.

My husband helped a great deal by arranging the music for the trio and did all the backing tracks, which made it possible for me to work with the singers. He rehearsed the singing group and practiced with us daily to harmonize together so we'd be a good enough to find work as a trio. Without my husband's help I couldn't have formed this type of singing group. While we were rehearsing the show, the contract arrived from Greece and I signed it for the Christmas period. I really thought things were improving and changing for me. When the tickets arrived for us to fly out to Greece ten days before Christmas, everything seemed to be going ok and the show was ready to start work. I felt an overwhelming sadness at that time of year leaving my family behind. Before the trouble started we'd always spent Christmas together and my husband and son had come out to join me wherever I was working. Now I was leaving them behind and the life that I'd previously had.

That life was coming to an end as my husband had already filed for a divorce and I'd agreed. The trust and closeness of our relationship had gone although we still ate and watched TV together for my son's sake. My married life was shattered although we remained friends right up to the end of my husband's life without bitterness. I do understand my husband could never accept what had happening to his wife. Being a very logical person, my husband wanted proof of what I said was happening to me. When I explained my condition he just couldn't grasp the situation and the trauma that it was causing me. He commented that my behavior was strange and totally out of character since I'd returned from Turkey. His advice to me was to get some medical help quickly as I'd been a normal person before the contract in Turkey... I hope by now the person whose is reading this book can understand what demon networks can create and do. With myself still being clueless of who the perpetrators were, demon gangs caused damage and excessive health issues while they remain inside my body.

I remember that day clearly when I left for Greece with my husband driving me to the airport to catch my flight. There had been a heavy snowfall the night before so we left extra early to get to the airport. The traffic to the airport was heavy and moving slowly because of the heavy snow that was still falling. It was close to Christmas and many people were heading for the airport and this made me wonder if the flight would be delayed due to the weather. The closer we got to the airport the heaver the traffic grew. It was a difficult journey travelling through the snow blizzard that was covering the roads which made me think we might end up being late and miss the flight.

I'd arranged to meet the two girl singers and dancers at the airport as I usually did with shows that were leaving for abroad. On arrival at the airport, there was no sign of any of the girl dancers. I went to look for them at the check-in desk. I walked around the area where we were supposed to meet and there was still no sign of them. Now it was getting late and reaching the time to board our flight.

I was frantic and went to phone them all up to see what had happened. Maybe they'd been delayed on their journeys through the bad weather or perhaps there had been an accident on the way to the airport. Finally, I got through to all the four girls only to be told that they'd decided to break the contract with me. They'd decided that they didn't want to be away from England at Christmas. This left me stuck at the Airport with two singers, a load of luggage and a contract that I'd already signed for a seven person show to start work in a few days' time in Greece. I didn't know what to do for the best. Should I board the plane and take a chance that I'd be able to get bookings for the trio or cancel the whole thing? I'd taken on a financial commitment with the bank to arrange the show and I needed to find work to repay the debt.

I decided to take a chance and board the plane for Greece with the singers. I spoke to both girls and explained the situation that we were in and they wanted to go to Greece. Neither of them had any other work lined up in England. Then I heard my own voice saying I'm sure we will find work for the trio once I've talked to the agent in Greece. At that moment in time I was stepping into an unknown destiny that might have me returning back to England quickly. When I boarded that flight I had no idea what lay ahead for the three of us.

Chapter 10

Greece with the Trio

Soon after I'd settled into my seat by the cabin window our plane gradually raced down the runway and took off. We were then lifted up into a white cloudless sky with a blizzard of snowflakes falling onto the plane. We gradually ascended higher into the swirling snow clouds, leaving England behind in the distance. I settled back into my seat for the journey that lay ahead but couldn't stop worrying about whether or not we'd find work for the trio in Greece. After about an hour, the blizzard became much heavier and snow was now covering the entire plane and cabin windows. Could the plane continue flying in such a blizzard?

While the snow continued falling, another chapter in my life was about to begin with the journey to Greece. Had my troubles with the supernatural world that had invaded mine finally been left behind? Since Ankara, had the suffering and turmoil gone or was it waiting to return and haunt me? I desperately needed a fresh start with the trio and hoped that I'd made the right choice by taking the flight to Greece. It was a journey into the unknown and I hoped we wouldn't be making a rapid return to England. If only I knew the answer?

I wasn't still feeling completely well with my health and worried in case the nightmarish condition should return. Ankara seems to have clung onto my life with its ongoing spiritual warfare of destruction which I desperately needed to be rid of to regain my life. Turkey felt like a magnet that kept drawing me back into its web of supernatural oblivion. I made another attempt to make myself comfortable in my seat and relax but this was impossible to achieve. Visions of the past year kept haunting me. I kept thinking about the club in Ankara, the paintings on the walls and Tarik. I was living in fear of the past and the unknown realms of darkness and its return. I felt deadly cold and shivery and I sensed that the Grim Reaper was close, waiting impatiently to strike my life with the sting of death which had touched several of my family members over the past year. Why did these morbid thoughts race around in my mind non-stop during that flight to Greece? I had been a victim of a devilish force which I knew was living off my flesh, blood and energy that brought chaos into my very existence.

I had no premonition when I signed the contract for Greece that things were going to get worse for me on this trip, or that I'd be returning to Turkey. During the rehearsals in England I'd felt slightly better and thought I might be on the road to recovery. On the flight to Greece I began to realize that I should have stayed in England longer as the voices were still with me. Suddenly the Captain's voice came across on the tannoy saying that due to the heavy snow fall, we'd be landing in Austria and spending the night there. Then he informed us that the airline company would be covering the expenses of the hotel and food for that night due to the weather condition being too dangerous to fly in. If the weather was clear the next day we'd be continuing our scheduled flight to Greece. He continued by saying that the airline would keep us updated on the situation.

We stayed in Austria overnight and left the next morning by bus for the airport as the weather had cleared up and it had stopped snowing. We flew to Greece and were met at the airport by the Greek agent who was far from happy with the delayed arrival. It was going to cause him quite a problem with the manager of the club whom I had signed the contract with for the Christmas period.

The agent didn't inform me right away that he didn't want us but said that he'd try and find us a job at another club as quickly as he could. I was really worried now as I'd only brought enough money with me to last until we started work. The girls had done the same, thinking that we'd be starting work in a few days. Being near Christmas, most of the clubs were already booked in advance with their acts and shows. Finding work for us in Greece was going to be difficult as there were plenty of singing acts available. While we waited to see if the agent found us a job, I kept the rehearsals going in our hotel room each day. We continued doing this for around twelve days but by then I was running out of money. As I had to pay for the three of us to eat and for anything else we needed each day until a job turned up.

Then one evening when we came back to the hotel after our evening meal, the agent called me to say that he'd found a job for the trio in Sera. He continued by telling me to have everything packed to leave the hotel in a couple of hours. He said to be ready on time as the manager of the club would be picking us up and travelling with us that evening. I repeated to the singers what the agent had said and told them to be ready to leave. I felt a great relief at the prospect of a job and knowing that we'd be starting work in a couple of days. Having this job would give us sufficient time to look for other engagements and call up other agents.

We were ready and waiting at the hotel when the manager from Sera arrived. It didn't take long for us to pack our costume trunks and personal luggage into his large car and start the journey down to Sera with him. We arrived late that evening and got settled in at the hotel. We did rehearsals the next day at the club and started work that night. The club was ok and we worked there over the Christmas period until the end of January. During that time, I called other agents to see if they could find some work for us from February onwards. I also called Mr. Macy in Turkey who I'd worked for in Ankara.

Turkey was the closest place to look for work and travel to from Greece. That was another big mistake that I made! I should have stayed away from Turkey. I was still suffering with the side effects from Ankara and hadn't fully recovered which meant I was taking a risk going back. I'm an optimist and thought things would be alright this time if we got a job there. I was desperate to find work for the trio as I'd bills to pay in England that couldn't wait. This gave me little choice in the matter but to look for another job so I wouldn't have to return to England still owing money. There was an air of deception in motion again drawing me back to Turkey to entrap me once more in its web.

The weeks we spent in Sera passed by quickly and the contract came to an end. I called the agent that we'd been working for to see if he had any other jobs for us. He told me he hadn't any job lined up. Now I had to search for work quickly to get a contract. That same day, Mr. Macy phoned me from Turkey to say that he'd found us a three month contract to work in Ankara. He gave me all the information about the job and told me about an overnight coach that went from Greece to Istanbul. Which would be the cheapest way to get there for the trio. If I wanted the job he'd arrange the work permits quickly for us. I agreed to the three month contract for Ankara then went ahead to make the arrangements for the journey and our departure from Greece.

Once I'd arranged everything, I went to see the agent that we'd been working for. When I mentioned to him that I was leaving Greece and had a contract for Turkey he became very aggressive, asking me to pay him commission for the jobs I would do there. What he suggested was ridiculous as he hadn't found the contract for us, Mr. Macy had. This work was nothing to do with him so I wasn't going to pay him any commission for the work in Turkey.

This gangster of an agent then began threatening me about what he was going to do if I went to Turkey and worked there. While I'd been in his office I'd been controlling myself, wishing to end with him peacefully. Now I had reached a point where I'd had enough of his crap and told him where to go. After doing this I knew there was one more problem to face. This was how to get the costume trunks out of his office. While I was thinking about this he asked me for the ticket money again which I'd just paid him while I was working in Sera. That had left me with very little money. This crook was aiming to bleed me dry before I left Greece. His next move was to hold the costume trunks as collateral. I brought the meeting in his office to an abrupt end when I slammed the door and walked out.

Then an idea came to me. It had to be carried out when he wasn't there. I'd have to ring the office first and check that he was out and have transport waiting to take the trunks straight to the coach station. I already had tickets for that evening and I'd have the girls waiting in the hotel ready to leave when I phoned to say I was on my way to pick them up. If my plans went ok we'd catch the night coach to Istanbul. At the coach depo I could ring Mr. Macy with our time of our arrival so he could be there to meet us off the coach in Istanbul. I'd worked around the world for many years with different agents and I knew the Greek agent was on the warpath for revenge. Things could get nasty and that's what worried me. If he suddenly showed up at the coach station he'd try to stop us from leaving. My plans had to be carried out to the last detail to work, so nothing could stop us from leaving on the coach as I'd already spent most of the money on the tickets.

As we were travelling by night to Istanbul I thought it would be fairly quiet. On our arrival at the coach station I was surprised to find crowds of people waiting to catch the night coach. Everyone on the coach had their own reasons why they need to be travelling through the night to reach their destinations in the city of a thousand mysteries. The three of us stood huddled together in the gloom of the coach station. I was nervous anticipating what might happen if we didn't catch the coach to Istanbul. In the semi-darkness I listened to the shrill cries of the street vendor's selling their wares to the passing throngs of people. Then we went to find the area where the coach for Istanbul was leaving from. We made our way there and joined the crowd of people waiting to board the coach.

Standing there I was feeling really tired and cold and wondered when the coach would arrive. My mind kept turning over all the events that I'd experienced from the past year since Ankara. Was everything going to be alright this time? Here I was, venturing and travelling into the unknown again. Ankara was the place where my story and ongoing nightmare first began just over a year ago. Were things going to be different this time around or would the supernatural power of darkness engulf me again with its evil manifestations and voices?

When I'd left England this time the snow had been falling and leaving a glimmering white glow everywhere it touched. Now in the dingy darkness of the coach station, the cold damp air and the shadows of the night were now closing in around us. I was edgy and growing more nervous by the minute. There was a certain déjà vu about this scene like I'd experienced it all before.

All of a sudden a large coach came into sight and swung in front of where we were standing. Its headlights glared on the waiting crowd as it came to a sudden halt in front of us. The driver got out of the coach and told us all to start lining up to board and then he began checking everyone's tickets. While this was going on I continued worrying about the Greek agent and if he should suddenly turn up and ruin everything for us to leave. While I was having all these negative thoughts and making myself really stressed out, our turn came in the queue to board the coach. Relief swept over me as the driver told us to put our luggage under the coach then board ourselves. We did this and boarded the coach and found our seats. We were now ready to leave for our overnight journey to Istanbul.

The driver put the key into the ignition and started the coach and our journey began. Once out of the coach depo we gradually picked up speed and got onto the main highway. Then we drove on through the darkness of night onwards towards our destination, Istanbul. I was crossing my fingers and hoping that my supernatural encounters were finally over. They'd been part of my existence for the past year and an unresolved mystery. We travelled throughout the night until eventually the darkness finally turned into the dawn of another new day. As Istanbul came into sight with people scurrying around doing their daily tasks. The sound of the early morning prayers being sang echoed from the mosques while we continued driving through the outskirts of Istanbul towards the coach station.

The next journey that I'd be taking would lead me back to Ankara where my bondage with the realms of darkness began. The place held many memories for me of events which had left lasting effects on my life. Returning to Ankara again made me wonder if I was doing the right thing. If my health continued to improve everything would be ok with the show and I'd be able to work the contract out. If the attacks returned I'd never get my life back on track.

On leaving England this time I had a legal two year separation from my husband. I'd also lost a lot of money plus had my ongoing health problems. We were now about to arrive and drive into the coach station in Istanbul where Mr. Macy would be waiting for us. Our coach drove into the depo and came to stop. We got out and I spotted Mr. Macy in the crowd waiting for us. He greeted me as usual with his ''Hello Irene'' and he told me that we'd be leaving for Ankara that evening by coach. He suggested that the three of us go and get something to eat and then go sit in his office and have a rest before our journey.

Chapter 11

Return to Ankara

It was the middle of January when we arrived in Ankara and it was very cold. We were met at the coach station by two of the waiters from the club who came to help us with the luggage and take us to the hotel where we'd be staying while we working in Ankara. The following day we rehearsed and started work at the club that night. We settled into a daily routine over the next few weeks. The club was situated quite centrally and within a short walking distance from our hotel. Our show went well on the opening night and the management were pleased with us. At last everything seemed to be going ok for the trio. I liked Ankara as it was a busy bustling place with enough shops to keep the girls occupied when they had money to spend having started work. Feeling optimistic about having a job for the next three months, I wanted to put all the negative experiences from Ankara and the past behind me.

Gradually I began to feel more confident about myself and the future in general. We rehearsed most days at the club to improve our routines and during these periods my health appeared to be better. I continued to feel more positive and optimistic about my future. Visiting the healers in England over the past months seemed to have restored my health to a certain degree which made me think that my past suffering was coming to an end. We'd been working at the club for about a month and I'd started to regain my old confidence back again working in show business, after all, it had always been my job.

Here it comes! Out of the blue one night Tarik came into the club with friends. This happened when I was on stage doing the show and I noticed a group of men who'd just arrived being shown to the two front tables near the stage. A bell rang in my head… it was ground hog day, yes it was! Tarik was like a ghost from the past who'd returned again on that night. He was out entertaining business clients as usual and had come into the club by chance where we happened to be working. This time when he came into the club Endless Love wasn't being played by the band. I was singing Don't Cry for Me Argentina with the girl backing-singers on stage. On seeing him I knew that he'd ask for the trio to join his table after the show, which he did.

When the three of us did this I noticed right away that Tarik was in a strange mood and his conversation turned to the past and Izmir in the 1970s. He began reminiscing about that time. Suddenly he took my hand in his and said that he'd regretted not telling me how he felt at that time ever since. If he had, things might have turned out differently for us both. He'd never felt quite the same about anybody since then and never married.

That evening he never stopped rambling on about the past and the compliments flowed on and on about my professional skills as an all-round entertainer. Next came my intelligence and loveliness as a woman. At that point I asked him if he'd been taking something. He assured me he hadn't but I was still wondering! No one could stop Tarik talking once he started! After work that night he offered to give the three of us a lift back to our hotel. On arrival at the hotel he didn't want to let me get out of the car. He grabbed my hand as I was getting out. I told him I couldn't repeat the same thing we'd been through the year before and went into my hotel with the girls. That was the last time I saw him in Ankara. Tarik's appearance that night seemed to open the doors for the attacks to begin once more. This time the demon network dug their claws into my body and life with a ferocious force!

The hellish state was back, tormenting my mind and body with another form of demonization. The effects and symptoms of it this time were a lot stronger than before. My horrific condition was back again and dragging me once more into the pits of despair and hopelessness. Instantaneously the 'feeling good' factor that I'd had about the future went and was replaced with fearful thoughts about my life and job for the second time around in Ankara. The boa constrictor was back wrapping itself around my body and life and squeezing the health out of my body. It clung onto me like a leach drawing blood from a person, that's how it felt to me. What I'd dreaded had returned with its soul- destroying effects to assault me once more.

Who'd understand how bad this condition is for a person who's suffering with it? You're being forced daily to battle on living with these attacks being made on you twenty four hours a day with no respite. This experience is horrendous to face each day and made worse by trying to hide away it from the world. I've had to do this most of the time since the 1980s when this condition invaded my life.

We were now half way through April and the contract would end in two weeks. I was still struggling on through each day as the attacks started being unleashed into me body and managing to cope with my job for the time being. However, the condition was causing me a great deal of mental and physical trauma. Being a practicing Christian didn't stop these horrific trials touching my life. Throughout all of them I held onto my faith during my darkest hours living with this experience.

I then signed a three month contract to work in Bursa at a club where I'd worked before. I was hoping that this contract would fit peacefully into my life without causing problems for the trio. During the last couple of weeks in Ankara, the voices became more constant. This was a worry for me. How was I going to cope if things got worse during the next contract? Being demonized is totally invisible to other people so you're alone suffering with this totally abnormal condition. No doctor would believe this could be happening to a person. I'm living proof that demonization does take place and happen to innocent people.

Chapter 12

We Arrive in Bursa

The journey down to Bursa was a long and tiring one and we arrived late afternoon and we were met as usual by waiters of the club. They took us to a hotel opposite a park where we'd be staying during our contract. While I was unpacking my cases and settling into my hotel room I felt slightly uneasy and didn't know why. The next thing I did was to phone the club to arrange rehearsals for the next day. At that moment I was feeling really tired after the journey as I hadn't slept the night before we travelled, I spent the rest of the day in the hotel trying to rest.

The following day we rehearsed at the club and while we were there I kept getting very heavy oppressive feelings that gradually made me feel ill at ease in the club. I thought it might be due to being overtired. That night we worked and the manager of the club was satisfied with our show. This made me feel optimistic that everything was going to turn out alright for the next three months.

My optimism was short-lived as after I'd been in Bursa for a few days my sleepless nights began to kick-in again. What I'm about to tell you now is a testimony of what happened to me and took place during the months that I spent working in Bursa. All the incidents that I mention did actually take place and happen to me. I'm describing them from how I perceived them at that time. Most of them were paranormal or supernatural manifestations which brought devastating effects to my health and wellbeing. What lay ahead for me over the next few months would surpass anything that I'd previously experienced with the condition. Which would gradually turn my hotel room in Bursa into a chamber of horrors over the next few months. When I began experiencing terrifying tortures and trials which were far worse than previously. These attacks became regular over the following weeks and my life began to turn into a full blown horror story.

I didn't know at the time that I was actually living with a stronghold of demons who were already inside my body and going to show me no mercy. Their atrocities would go on undetected by human eyes during that summer in Bursa. Which caused my health to deteriorate at a rapid pace through the stress that the condition brought with it. My sleepless nights were back with non-stop disturbances from the attacks. Along with brainwashing from the voices being filtered into my mind over the following weeks, my symptoms of bodily aches and pains that I thought had gone returned. From then onwards I was just having brief periods of sleep during the night. Those periods were filled with night terrors and bad dreams which haunted me. I'd suddenly wake up exhausted after another sleepless night. My horrors of the past year were back, plaguing my body again.

Whenever I went to bed I knew that I'd be spending another night tossing and turning unable to sleep being terrorized by the perpetrators from hell. What had returned was sadistic warfare aiming to destroy my body and mind even further this time round. I didn't realize how bad my situation was going to get over the next few months. Through being terrorized non-stop, I started suffering with ongoing depression and the hopelessness of not being able to resolve what was happening to me again. Everywhere I went in Bursa seemed to give me an eerie unsettled feeling of being watched by unseen eyes that seemed to follow me everywhere I went. These feelings always seemed stronger whenever I was alone in the hotel. During those times the atmosphere would become electrifying and oppressive. Something strange and supernatural seemed to linger in all the corridors of the hotel that was inexplicable.

After I'd been in a Bursa a couple of weeks a dancer who'd previously worked for me who was now settled and living there heard that I was working at the casino and came to see me at the hotel. It was towards the end of May by then when Jenny came to visit me. She suggested that it was an ideal time to start going to the beach which wasn't too far away. The summer had begun now with the heat beginning to engulf Bursa. Jenny mentioned that her boyfriend wouldn't mind taking all three of us to the beach when they went. I spoke to the girls and they thought it was a good idea. About a week later Jenny came to see me again and we planned when we'd start going to the beach together. I really needed a break from work and the hotel so the beach seemed an ideal place to get away to.

May turned into June and the weather became extremely hot. The hotel had no air condition so the rooms were clammy with heat. During that time I was having terrible sensations with movements inside my body along with the voices going on constantly, that was beginning to drive me nuts. Not being able to sleep at night was draining my energy and making me tired all the time. The intensive heat of June didn't help matters as I knew it would continue on for the next few months. All I wanted to do was get out of that hotel and go to the beach whenever Jenny's boyfriend could take us.

I was grateful for those days and to be out in the sunshine and fresh air which generally made me feel a lot better. It seemed to calm down what I was experiencing inside my body. Once I was in the sea water at the beach I could briefly relax. However, the hotel was beginning to feel like a prison that I desperate needed to escape from. The supernatural phenomenon was haunting me now non-stop wouldn't leave me alone. During that time I was reaching breaking point again through the nightly sadistic battering of my body. The beach seemed to alleviate some of my suffering being in a different atmosphere and out in the open air. Those days we spent at the beach always seemed to pass quickly and made me feel better just being away from that hotel with different company.

Usually when we arrived at the beach we'd find a spot near the water's edge and put our belongings down. Then one of us would stay with them while the rest went off for a swim or paddled around in the water. This way, everyone got a turn and a chance to do whatever they wanted to. We always took a picnic lunch with us to share. Usually after lunch we'd swim or go for a walk down the beach. The rest of the afternoon was spent chatting and enjoying sunbathing until it was time to pack up and return to Bursa. We usually got back to the hotel in the late afternoon which gave us plenty of time to shower and have a rest before the long night at the club.

On our second visit to the beach for some unknown reason I started collecting shells that were shaped like minarets. The shells were scattered all over the beach we were on that day. While I was collecting shells, everyone came to join me and help. Suddenly in the middle of doing this, the atmosphere changed into a weird and strange one. When this took place everyone went into a frenzy of collecting shells with aggressive arguing starting about who'd collected the most shells. It was ridiculous and turning nasty. While this was going on I felt a cold chill pass over my entire body on that steaming hot day. Then I got the weird feeling again that we were all being watched by unseen eyes which were out there somewhere.

The beach was fairly deserted that day apart from a couple of families with children who were enjoying their day by the sea. I decided to take a walk along the beach to get some exercise and peace to clear my head. Walking along the edge of the sea the water was warm as it gently covered my feet while the rays of sunlight filtered into my body. Still being early afternoon the beach was fairly empty as most people avoided the heat and came later. The group I was with were gradually left behind in the distance as I walked on.

I could still see Jenny and her boyfriend sunbathing, Jane paddling in the water and Patsy lying sunbathing reading one of her romantic novels. When I reached the far end of the beach I stopped to admire nature at its best. The view was amazing with the sun's reflection on the water as it changed the sea into a brilliant gold as the bright rays of sunlight touched the water. It was an awesome scene to watch as I turned around and began to walk back to the group. This time I went a little deeper into the sea until the water came up around my knees. It felt hot and soothing as my feet sank deeper into the sand below the surface of the water where the sea became shallower.

Feeling calmer now I began to walk back down the beach to join the others. Then out of nowhere my peaceful mood disappeared into a fearful one. There was a strange stillness on the beach that day like the calm before the storm. My storm came with an outburst of sadistic attacks from the pits of hell a few days later.

During those moments on the beach I felt an overwhelming fear and tension return. What was happening to me I just didn't know… it was overtaking my life once more. The peace that I'd briefly experienced was now dissolving rapidly into a sea of worry. I didn't want to return to the hotel and my room, the thought of being alone there terrified me. Walking back towards the group on the beach I noticed a wooded area that would make a perfect spot to watch the group from. It was close to a number of buildings that were directly opposite to where we were located on the beach. There was also a coffee bar where anyone could have watched us from. The thoughts that I kept having were absurd that someone was watching us but at that time I was distraught and stressed out and didn't know what was happening to me.

Although that day was very hot I kept feeling cold and fearful about returning to Bursa. I shivered as an unknown fear clung onto me. My premonition that something awful was about to take place that would carry me into a vortex of horrors which I would have to battle with to survive. The feelings that I kept having turned into a reality over the next few weeks after the visit to the beach.

Looking back now on what happened to me in Ankara and Bursa, I understand now that it wasn't being done to me by a person but by the gang of demons. They were already residents inside my body and causing all the disruption and illness. These perpetrators had been creating all the horrific ordeals that I'd been experiencing since the beginning of my arrival in Ankara. Sensing fear of the unknown was now a familiar issue that confronted me daily. During those periods I was wrestling with the principalities and powers from the world of darkness. They were my reality now that I was forced to live with them on a daily basis. The condition was now at a very dangerous stage for my health and whole existence was at risk if it didn't end. Having a demon stronghold living inside your body jeopardizes your life.

Every day I grew more frantic and worried about what was going to happen to me next. I felt constantly haunted everywhere I went. They were there in the shadows of the corridors of the hotel waiting and hovering around me, tormenting and dragging me deeper into a state of no return. The nightly attacks were leaving me in a totally oblivious state trying to figure out why this abuse was taking place and happening to me. Then the signs and symptoms of a pending nervous breakdown began taking place in my body as I couldn't take anymore abuse. When I returned to England after Bursa I had a nervous breakdown. My experience in Turkey was one of sheer torture and terrorization of the highest degree that would have driven any person insane. Demonization is a hellish condition for anyone to have and live through that leaves behind lasting scars that you can't erase.

During the last few weeks in Bursa I existed in a zombie-type of state most of the time, still being attacked and suffering sadistic abuse night after night. This condition brought a terrible feeling of oppression and bondage for me having had it for so long. That's an Anti-Christ act that's was done against me as a free person. A demon uses every orifice of a person's body and to abuse a victim more and more as the condition intensifies. This became unbearable for my body to cope with and bear. The attacks caused a nervous trembling condition to take place throughout my body that I couldn't control through my nervous system which malfunctioned. Having this alien affliction is horrific for anyone to experience. It's soul-destroying to put up with as it's with you twenty four hours a day with no respite.

While I was at the club I was still being bombarded with the issue on and off throughout the evenings while I was working with my show. My daily life felt like I was living on the edge of a precipice hanging on to each day uncertain of what will come next. When I left England I had thought my condition had nearly gone but it had never been taken away completely from my body but was lying dormant inside me, biding its time to raise its serpents head and attack me. Demonization is similar to having a python attack you as it coils itself around your body and life. In Bursa it wanted to squeeze my life entirely out of me and drive me insane. In the beginning I kept hoping that I'd wake up one day and find my nightmare gone but that's not how it works with the enemy.

Chapter 13

The Nightly Horrors Begin

That's why I took the decision to tell Jenny and Amir about what I was suffering with the next time they came to visit me. I did this a few days later when Jenny and Amir came to see me at the hotel and I told them about everything that had been happening to me for the past year since Ankara. Both of them listened intently to everything that I said about my supernatural problems and about how they'd resurfaced since my arrival in Bursa. Amir appeared to believe what I'd told them both and said that he'd heard other stories that were similar to mine. I thought that I'd be more protected working in Bursa because it was a religious town but that didn't seem to be the case.

Amir continued by explaining to me that certain people were still practicing a form of magic which was being used to ruin peoples bodies and lives. The magic was kept secret but still being used undercover. After being given this information it seemed evident to me that more people could be suffering with what I was experiencing.

Bursa opened another door into a dimension of horrors that I'd like to tell you about which took place during that long hot summer when I was working there. When my hotel room became my prison with manifestations and ongoing evil incidents. One night after going to bed I was suddenly woken up by the sound of someone screaming. It sounded like the person was being beaten up and in pain. I opened the door of my room to see where the noise was coming from. On doing this a deathly silence descended over the floor that I lived on and the noise stopped completely. I checked all the rooms that were close to mine and they were all silent with no sign of anyone on the floor that I lived on.

The following day another weird incident took place when the sheets of my bed were being changed in my room by the hotel maids. On touching the sheets while the bed was being made, I noticed that they were wet and complained to the maid. She looked viciously directly at me and said they were dry in English. Then she told me in Turkish that I was crazy. Later that day I reported the incident to the management but they did nothing to the hotel maid about this incident.

Throughout the coming weeks more weird and strange supernatural incidents just continued going on non-stop daily. Another night I'd been in bed for a couple of hours when I was woken up again. This time I could hear the sound of a ball being bounced on the floor of the room above mine. The noise went on for a few hours non-stop and it was definitely coming from the room above mine. In the morning I mentioned the incident to the hotel receptionist who just laughed and told me that there was no one living in that room above mine, it was empty.

When I saw Amir again he offered to take me to see someone who might be able to help me with what I was experiencing. The person lived within a short distance from Bursa. Jenny offered to go with me. If only I'd taken up their offer to see someone it might have stopped the terrible ordeal that I was suffering with which was about to become far worse to deal with alone. Over the next couple of weeks my life gradually turned into a limbo state living with the condition. The ongoing attacks with trials and tortures gradually became more terrifying by the day. During this stage I felt trapped in my own body and totally helpless to stop what was being done to me physically and mentally. What took place a few weeks later made me regret not taking Amir's offer up to get some help

During another one of these attacks on a different night I suddenly heard the sound of a bell being rung in the distance. Then I heard voices chanting some type of ritual that sounded similar to a mass of some type. I could hear all this quite clearly although it was somewhere in the distance. This chanting went on for some time then stopped suddenly. Then the brainwashing with the voices and the torments began again. After an attack I'd be lying awake in a traumatic state for hours until the first light of dawn came through the cracks of the blinds of my room.

Being deprived of sleep most nights my energy level was low and I was starting to feel 'phased out' all the time. Sleeping now was a thing of the past and a rare event. If I slept at all now I'd be having dreams with different terrifying scenarios with strange undertones from the past with Tarik and that day trip to Zelve. I was also being haunted with dreams of my family and their suffering through what had happened to me in Turkey. How could I rest or sleep with all these traumatic things going on non-stop? These attacks were now ongoing and didn't cease night after night... so what rest or peace could I get with all this going on?

During this whole period I continued doing my nightly routine when I returned to the hotel after work each night. I had a shower my usual cup of tea and a light snack, read for a short time and then went to bed hoping to get some rest and sleep. Each night I tried to dismiss what was going on inside my body and made every attempt to sleep but the task of achieving this was impossible. There wasn't a moment's peace at that time, it was just ongoing suffering and mental stress.

Another night I'd gone to bed and slept for a brief period when I was jolted awake suddenly. This time I woke up with pains on my face and shoulder areas. It felt like something was being thrown at me like stones as the blows kept hitting my face and shoulders. Being woken up suddenly I was in a catatonic state of fear and couldn't move. What in God's name was happening to me now? Now I was being brutalized sadistically by this alien force who were holding me hostage and attacking me. Who or what was doing this to me?

I must have blacked out with the pain and shock. I know now that it was being done to me by the perpetrators from hell who're were inside my body. I'd no idea at that time who or what was doing this to me. When I came to and opened my eyes I began to experience terrible chest pains like a heart attack until I finally came around for the second time and opened my eyes. My face and shoulder areas were really hurting now and it was difficult for me to get out of bed. I did and went to look in the mirror and I was shocked when I saw my reflection.

My face and shoulder areas looked as though they'd been badly beaten or punched and had black and bluish marks. Still in shock I stared at my reflection in the mirror feeling sick. Then my stomach began to rumble and I vomited. What in God's name was happening to me? Taking my bible off the bedside cabinet I pressed it down on all the bruised areas on my face and shoulders. Then I pressed it on my head which was feeling like it was going to split in two. Calling out to God in desperation, I asked him to stop my terrible nightmare. To be honest, I didn't expect anything to happen but felt helpless and alone living with this ongoing horror in my life. I'd asked for God's help with faith and was answered.

After pressing the bible down on all the bruised areas, they gradually appeared to fade away. While this was taking place I fainted and when I came round I'd no recollections of what had taken place and I was lying on the bed. What I've written here is all I remember. My mind was muddled up at that point and I didn't even know what day or year it was. After making several attempts to get up off the bed, I couldn't because I felt too weak. About an hour later I finally managed to pull myself up. After doing this I put my dressing gown on and went down the corridor to the girl's room to ask them some questions about the previous night.

When I knocked on their door it was answered by one of the girls. Then I questioned them both briefly about the previous night when we'd all returned to the hotel together after work. Both girls looked at me puzzled and I could see by their expressions that they were trying hard not to laugh. I could see they both thought that I was heading for the nut house the way things were going or a nervous breakdown.

After that night of terror I began to use my bible as a form of protection, whenever I was being attacked by enemy. Through my own experience of living with demonic networks I know that they definitely exist. They will show no pity for anyone who becomes their victim. This type of terrorization will continue until a person's is freed from this type of bondage. Demons come from the realms of darkness and this is an Anti-Christ act and a terrible affliction for any person to suffer with.

It must have been about a week later when I saw Tarik for the last time. This event in Bursa was very similar to what happened previously in Ankara when he made an unexpected appearance. I'd noticed a large group of men being shown to the front tables while we were doing our show which gave me an odd feeling that it might be Tarik on a night out entertaining business people. While I was singing I tried to stay calm so as not to ruin my performance that night. After our show while we were changing in the dressing room and there was a knock on the door. I opened the door to find a waiter standing there who told me that the trio had been invited to join the front table. My intuition had been right, it was Tarik with the group of men.

Once the waiter had gone we changed into our evening clothes and the three of us went to join the group at the front table. Here it comes! When we joined the table the orchestra began to play their interpretation of Endless Love with the singer 'killing' the song's lyrics. While this was going on all the men around the table stood up as we joined them with the usual courtesy to greet us which made me think another chapter in my life was about to begin that might sort out the past and the turbulent friendship between Tarik and myself. I noticed straight away that Tarik was in an amiable mood and didn't mention anything about the past incident between us in Ankara.

That night he was entertaining guests in his world who mattered to him. He was playing the charming host to his business associates and he was out to impress them. The first comment he made to me as I joined the table was how well I looked, then a compliment about how much he'd enjoyed the new singing group and our show. Looking back on that evening so long ago, I realize Tarik was an expert at keeping his emotions well-hidden and under control. He managed this task well along with his impeccable good manners.

While we were together that evening, Tarik never mentioned anything about the day trip to Zelve which left me wondering for many years if he had experienced anything strange since that day? I'd heard a rumor while I was still working in Ankara from someone that he'd never let me go which made me wonder if he'd had something to do with what was happening to me? That evening in Bursa was the last time that I would ever see Tarik when he left the club in an amiable mood with his group.

Then a few years later Tarik did turn up again but this time in England. It was a surprise to me because I'd never given him my phone number but he'd managed to get hold of it somehow. He phoned me and asked me to meet him at the hotel where he was staying for a few days while he was in England as he needed desperately to talk to me. I never went to meet him as I was going through a terrible period with my life at home and didn't want to get him involved with my problems. I've regretted this ever since over the years as he might have been able to resolve part of my story.

Let me continue now by telling you the rest of my story and what took place next while I continued working with the trio after that night when Tarik came into the club. We were in June now and I was still managing to keep a positive outlook about finishing the contract although I was still worried about how I was going to keep coping without getting sufficient sleep at night. Over the days that followed I started feeling continuously ill but clung onto the idea that I'd finish the contract. I was positive but my days were numbered as nightly attacks grew and became horrendous, dragging me deeper into the depths of despair until they finally turned into an unmanageable state that I couldn't handle or cope with any longer.

With only two weeks left to finish the contract the inevitable took place due to the constant stress of being demonized. I collapsed under the pressure and had to stop working and never finished the contract. My condition gradually manifested into a full blown health horror. The violation of my body began to cause frequent black outs and giddiness to take place. Then my health started to deteriorate rapidly through the continuous nightly battering and the lack of sleep. During that time I was walking about in a dazed comatose state daily with pains in my entire body. I was chronically ill the last few weeks as the attacks became more violent and sadistic affecting me both mentally and physically. I knew I was going to collapse completely if it didn't stop. Being physically weak with no energy I was on the verge of the nervous breakdown which did happen when I returned to England after Bursa.

Being demonized is an abomination for any human being to survive, it's a totally soul destroying act. This conditions has been a nightmare for me having had it for so many years and is something I haven't been able to escape or wake up from. Living with this issue continuously has turned my life into an oppressed limbo state. This supernatural world of spiritual wickedness with demons is a frightful situation to find yourself existing in. It became my reality.

In Bursa I was growing more lethargic and weak. My body went haywire under the strain. I'd reached a point where I couldn't take any more suffering. The effects of the attacks had left me living in a hellish state, feeling trapped in my own body. I was being used continuously as a host and a battering rod by demons. And as a pawn in their game of evil against religion and God, they were using my body and life. I never realized how horrifying my ordeal was going to materialize into being held a captive with this type of bondage. My last few days in Bursa were spent living in a confused and dazed state. The place left permanent stigmata on my entire life and body that's never stopped haunting my life ever since.

Chapter 14

Torments and Tortures

What took place next came through being held a prisoner with the condition in my body, and through the amount of stress it was causing me. It had become unbearable. Then one afternoon when I was left alone in the hotel I snapped and went berserk. Not having slept for days on end I'd reached breaking point and got hysterical, I just couldn't take anymore. My judgement was clouded and muddled at the time when this incident took place. I'd been under a great deal of stress with the voices going on all that afternoon and believed what the voices said to be true.

The voices told me I was being held a prisoner in the hotel and couldn't leave. I lost control, went berserk. I started screaming and shouting hysterically and then opened the windows of my room and threw my suitcases out into the street. Why did I do such a crazy thing as logically no one could stop me leaving the hotel if I wanted to? This is just an example of what the non-stop voices can create by continuously plaguing a person. When this incident took place I was being tormented twenty four hours a day.

This would drive any sane person into doing abnormal things and can easily happen once a demonic gang gets hooked into the wavelength of your mind. The outcome of your actions can be devastating when this type of situation takes place. The principalities of darkness and spiritual warfare intended to drive me to the brink of insanity and they nearly did. Demons thrive on tormenting a victims mind and body with various different situations until you're driven to a point of no return. A trained exorcist is well aware of what demonization and possession can create in a person's mind and body once a demon takes up residence inside a person.

On that day in Bursa the tormenting voices had driven me to desperation when I threw my suitcases out of the hotel window. I cried out to God to help me! Then a few seconds later an earth tremor hit the whole of Bursa and the hotel shook violently. While the tremor was taking place my door burst open and the girls who worked with me came rushing into my room screaming to tell me what was happening. Did the tremor just happen by chance or were my cries for help heard by God? That's puzzled me until this day.

During that time I was existing between two worlds, mine and the supernatural one. My condition had now become extremely hard to cope with as I was getting very little rest or sleep during the day or night because my mind was being bombarded with various alien events each time I attempted to sleep. Amir had offered to get me help but I'd failed to notice the seriousness of my condition and did not realize how much worse it could get. We were in the middle of June now and my room was hot and humid.

I pulled the blinds down hoping it would keep the sun out and cool the room down. I lay down on top of the bed to see if I could get a short rest and drifted off into a traumatized sleep, with the murmuring voices and the occasional demonic movement's still taking place inside me. While I rested in this disturbed sleep I visualized three crosses and then the voices began again. This time they began tormenting me with a religious type of trial saying that they were going to crucify Pope John Paul, Mother Teresa and they needed me to suffer the experience that Christ went through on the cross. During this trial a strange sinister mass was being sung that I could hear clearly. What was being done to me was another Anti-

Christ ordeal and I was being used as a scapegoat for religion. I started having terrible pains throughout my body that were being done to me by the stronghold of demons inside me.

On that day Pope John Paul was shot by a Turkish man, another strange coincidence while I was being tortured in Turkey with the trial of the crosses. Once again I was left traumatized and in pain wondering why these attacks were happening to me. Was it because I'm a Christian? Then the visions of the crosses gradually began to fade and the mass voices became whispers and were gone. Still lying on the bed, I began to tremble violently and couldn't stop. I felt freezing cold again on that hot summers day after that mind blowing encounter with the supernatural world of evil.

Chapter 15

Bloodbath and Tears

What came next was the most terrifying ordeal that I experienced in Bursa. On that particular night I'd returned to the hotel after work feeling somewhat exhausted. I hadn't felt well all evening at the club but hadn't mentioned anything to the girls who I worked with. I did the show that night and managed to carry on coping the best I could for the rest of the evening, hoping that I'd gradually feel better. When I got back to the hotel, all I wanted to do was rest and sleep. Every night when I came in from work there was always a tray waiting for me to collect at the reception desk to take up to my room. That night it was there as usual with Turkish tea and toast. I took the tray and went up to my room.

When I reached the room I showered, read for a short awhile then went to bed, hoping to get a good night's sleep... but that didn't happen. I'd only been in bed for a short time when an attack began with lots of physical abuse, brainwashing and abusive torments being done to my entire body that went on endlessly. It was impossible for me to sleep once the attack began. What I experienced that night was the worse manifestation of supernatural sadistic abuse. I made various attempts to try and stop the abuse but without success.

The abuse continued for hours that night until I was finally cocooned into an oblivious state with terrible pains in my entire body and feeling faint. Then I just seemed to be sinking into a never ending vortex of darkness. I must have blacked out, I don't know how long I was in that state. When I came to after the attack and opened my eyes, I was propped up against the wall of the bathroom shower, sitting in the basin. With no idea of how I'd got there or what had happened to me?

Still in a dazed state, I turned my head slightly and saw the bloody mess in the shower and on me. Then I felt the warm sticky blood on my legs and saw that I was still bleeding from my inside. There was blood all around me in the shower basin where I was still sitting in shock, propped up against the wall. Still in a catatonic state as I looked down and saw that I was surrounded with my own blood and sitting in it. I made a wild attempt to move and get up but felt faint again. The blood was now running down the bottom half of my body onto my legs. Then I noticed that blood was spattered everywhere in the shower. I was in shock, felt dizzy and faint and started to tremble violently again. When I touched my face it was wet with blood too. My legs were shaking now and I wondered if I'd ever be able to stand up. Feeling very weak, I just continued sitting in the shower for quite a time until I could manage to stand up. When I finally did I went to take a look in the bathroom mirror.

Seeing my reflection in the mirror made me even more nauseous. I looked at my face it was smeared with blood and my eyes held a haunted stare like a caged animal. My tormented reflection gazed back at me in total despair. God do something to help me! Despair and tears of hopelessness took over and I began to cry and couldn't stop the tears just flowed. Why was this happening to me? I just didn't understand who was battering my body and ruining my entire life. How could I stop this nightmare of violence and abuse? Nausea swept over me again and I was sick. Then I was gasping for air and shivering and feeling deadly cold. I remember looking down at the nightdress that I was wearing. It was clinging onto my body like a grotesque robe covered with sticky red blood. The perpetrators of this abuse had left their mark of venom and their calling card. The stigmata of that night was left imprinted on my body and soul. What had happened to me during that time lapse? I remember being attacked and feeling ill then drifting into an overwhelming darkness that engulfed me... then nothing more.

When I was finally able to get myself up I stood under the shower in a dazed state and turned the water on full blast. I watched the water as it poured over my body, washing the blood into watery circles around my feet. I felt hypnotized standing in the shower staring at the blood until it was washed away. Still shaking, I washed myself several times and shampooed my hair to remove the vile abuse which I'd experienced that night. I was still finding it hard to believe what was happening to me... it was totally abnormal. Still traumatized and feeling nauseous, I vomited again and then had to lie down on the bed as I felt really ill. Then I felt faint with a sinking feeling that was overwhelmed by darkness at that point and I must have passed out.

When I woke up and looked at my alarm clock on the bedside cabinet it was nearly midday. The sunlight was filtering into the room through the gaps in the shutters. The heat in my room was unbearable with very little fresh air coming in. My head ached and I still felt dizzy as I tried to get up but couldn't. The stifling heat in my room was overpowering and I had to remain lying on the bed for some time. While I lay there I kept replaying the scene in the bathroom with blood everywhere. The sadistic abuse of that attack had left terrible psychological and physical effects with me that I couldn't erase.

My emotional condition took over again and I began to cry endless tears of despair and hopelessness. I couldn't take any more of this torments and abuse! It took me quite a while to control my emotions but I knew that I still had to clean up the bloody mess that still clung to the bathroom walls. I felt like collapsing again and my heart was beating violently in my chest. I still felt dazed and confused about what was going on. And desperately needed someone to confide in but there was no one to turn to. I was alone in my prison cell in that hotel.

Feeling totally isolated living with my ongoing terrifying nightmare. The condition was now harming me both mentally and physically as it became a permanent fixture in my life until I could find a way to rid myself from it. Living with this supernatural phenomenon of horrors had now become my reality that I was being forced to endure. I'd felt too ashamed to bring the hotel staff or the girls to my room to witness the scene in the bathroom. That's why I cleaned it up myself. My head was pounding with pain again as I undertook the task of cleaning up the bathroom. How could I survive in this macabre world of darkness that wouldn't stop haunting me?

After the bathroom incident things grew worse for me to cope with and the girls who worked with me had lost interest in listening to my supernatural problems. I could see they didn't believe a word of what I was saying although both girls agreed that I looked ill and needed to see a doctor and get some help.

Over the following days I kept worrying and questioning myself about how I'd got into the bathroom and in the shower. Why was I wearing a different nightdress from the one that I'd gone to bed in that night? Had I got up and changed my nightdress during the attack myself? Had something been put in my tea that I'd taken from the reception desk that night…had I been drugged? The next question that came to my mind was had I been raped as there was a lot of blood everywhere? Or maybe I'd been used in some type of sacrificial ritual like I'd been told was still going on!

After the bloody bathroom incident I showered, dressed and then sat on the bed for a few minutes to rest. I was planning to go and talk with the girls about the previous night. While I was sitting on the bed suddenly the door of my room opened and a waiter came in without knocking carrying a tray of breakfast. I hadn't ordered breakfast because I felt sick and eating was the last thing that I wanted to do. He'd surprised me…how had he got into my room without a pass key? Who'd told him to bring me breakfast? When I tried to question the waiter he replied that he didn't speak English although he'd understood what I'd just asked him. Without speaking to me again, he put the breakfast tray down quickly on the bedside cabinet and left rapidly, closing the door behind him. Then he disappeared down the corridor. I heard the swishing sound of the lift going down and I assumed the waiter was in it. I'd always locked my hotel door at night and now I felt even more vulnerable being in the situation that I was living in.

How could I prove that these strange supernatural incidents were actually taking place in my body and life? I needed some sort of proof for myself. I went down to the girl's room to question them about the previous night when we'd returned to the hotel together after work. Both girls confirmed that they'd heard me locking my door. Something was going on in the hotel it wasn't all in my imagination… it was happening to my body and life. Who'd committed this horrific act of abuse? Now I was frightened of being left alone in my hotel room in the daytime or at night.

That day I phoned Jenny and explained to her what had taken place. She advised me to remain calm and that she'd be over to see me later in the day with her boyfriend. When Jenny came to the hotel that day she told me to let her know if things got worse. If they did, she said that I could go and stay with them for a few days. I couldn't stop thinking and worrying about all the terrible things that were happening to me after Jenny and her boyfriend left. I glanced at my alarm clock it was nearly midday and the heat was stifling as it filled the room. My head was throbbing and I still felt phased out and could hardly breathe as the stifling heat engulfed the room and I felt faint. Although I felt ill my mind was racing around with a will of its own, trying to recollect the time lapse of missing hours that I couldn't account for or remember which had left me bleeding in the shower. Where were these vicious attacks of violence coming from?

What would happen to me next in this hotel of horrors, would I survive this nightmare of ongoing attacks? My mind just kept recalling the bathroom scene and the appalling state that I'd been in with me having no recollection of how I'd got there or of what had taken place. Through my own years of experience living with networks of demons, I know now that these acts which I've suffered with were being done to me by them. In Bursa I didn't know this fact and the painful memories from that place have been left imprinted in my mind. The condition never completely ended but has clung onto my existence throughout the years.

Chapter 16

Leaving Bursa

After the bleeding attack incident I never regained my health and remained in a weak physical state with the condition until I left Bursa. Although I was feeling pretty ill most of the time, I still wanted to cope and continue working. The club was quite near the hotel where we were staying so every night we walked to work. On this particular night we set out as usual from the hotel to walk down to the club. I'd only walked a short distance when I suddenly felt like I was being hit on the head with a heavy object. The sensation of the blows to my head gradually grew worse as the pain increased until I started feeling dizzy and faint, then I collapsed in the street. I couldn't stand up. I just kept sinking deeper into a pit of darkness which I had no control of. While the girls who worked with me kept asking me to try and get up I couldn't as every part of my body had no strength. I was shaking uncontrollably and didn't know what was going on or happening to me. The girls propped me up with something and left me lying on the pavement for some time. Eventually I managed to stand up and supported by them walked very slowly back to the hotel. When we got there the receptionist helped up me up to my room where I stayed for the next few days.

After collapsing in the street I kept having blacking out spells whenever I felt nervous or confused about what was happening to me. During those times I felt like a zombie living between two different worlds the supernatural one with voices and torments and my own (which I was trying so desperately to hold onto).

Not going to work that night caused a lot of trouble at the club which left me no alternative but to end the contract. My health had reached a critical stage and I knew that I was too ill to continue working. I'd reached a point with the condition where I needed to return home to England quickly to get some medical help. I spent the last few days in Bursa with Jenny and her boyfriend at their house which made me feel a lot safer than being in the hotel. The entire three months that I'd spent working in Bursa were the worst that I'd ever experienced or lived through with this horrendous condition.

Throughout the last week before we left Bursa I was walking around in a comatose dazed and confused state. During that time I packed up and made all the travel arrangements to leave for England. I tried to keep everything going to schedule and appearing 'normal' but my health and wellbeing were in a terrible state. That finally led to a nervous breakdown on my return to England. Two men who the girls knew offered to drive us to Istanbul airport to catch our flight to England.

The day of departure arrived and the three of us were busy getting our baggage down from our rooms into the hotel foyer to leave. The manager of the hotel appeared suddenly carrying a large bunch of flowers that he said were for me from an admirer. He was about to hand the flowers to me when I noticed that they were blood red roses.

That day I wasn't feeling well and thought the roses were just another bad omen and I told the manager to give the flowers back to the sender. Looking back on the incident now the flowers were just sent at the wrong time. I was stressed out with the situation that

I was going through and thought that everything was sent to harm me.

That hotel had become a form of asylum for me through being terrorized non-stop by the principalities of darkness. All I wanted to do was to get as far away from the place as I could. The hosts of spiritual wickedness do exist and I've met and lived with them also experienced their many torturers in that hotel. That's why I can confirm that demonic strongholds are still entering peoples bodies in the world that we live in.

The men who were taking us to Istanbul arrived on time to pick us up with two cars. When they arrived I was already in a tense state and just wanted to leave for Istanbul as quickly as possible. Jenny and her boyfriend arrived at the hotel to say their good-byes to us and they were about the only good thing that happened to me by meeting them again in Bursa.

Although I felt happy to be leaving Turkey I was dreading returning home to England. I had health issues again and was still suffering with the demonization. I was also extremely worried about how my husband would react to me being ill again when I returned home. With our pending divorce now in motion, my whole life seemed to be messed up along with my health. Yes I was worried about what the outcome would be.

The luggage was now loaded into the two cars and we were ready to leave for Istanbul. When the car doors were slammed shut I was hoping that my troubles would be left behind in Bursa. Then an overbearing foreboding came over me as we left the hotel behind in the distance that my prison sentence with the condition wasn't over yet.

We'd been driving for some time when I began having violent pains in my stomach and abdomen. Then I started bleeding internally for some unknown reason. When this happened I asked the men who were driving us to Istanbul if we could stop and find a pharmacy and a toilet as quickly as possible. With no alternative left I had to explain what my problem was to the men. They were extremely helpful and understanding and told me not to worry and found what I needed quickly. We then continued our journey to Istanbul. Believe me, these two men were angels sent to help us that day. They took the utmost care of the three of us for the whole journey.

The last stop we made before reaching Istanbul was at a self-service bar to use the toilets and have something to drink. Once we got out of the cars we were suddenly surrounded by a crowd of aggressive people who seemed to appear out of nowhere. They were acting and behaving in a vicious manner as they came towards us. Then they began to surround us and began spitting and swearing insults at us. The men who were with us pushed the people away as they came closer, trying to hit us. It was a terrifying situation that we found ourselves in with a violent crowd behaving this way towards us. During this confrontation the men never ceased standing between us and the crowd to prevent us getting hit. One of the men told us to go the toilet quickly and then return to the cars while the other man kept pushing the people away from us.

We ran to the toilets, returned to the cars, got in and slammed the doors shut. Once we were inside the car and on the way to Istanbul I noticed how badly shaken the man who was driving our car was by the incident we'd all just been through. Both men had seemingly kept calm throughout the whole ordeal and dealt with the situation. There was an overpowering silence in the car and the atmosphere felt tense and eerie. It felt like the hosts of wickedness were waiting to touch and strike everything that I came into contact with.

The uncanny silence lingered on for some time until the man who was driving the car that I was in spoke to me about the incident. He said the people were fanatics that hated visiting foreigners and they had seen us getting out of the cars and guessed what we were. That's why they'd surrounded us, screaming abusive insults and spitting at us. They were just protesting against us being in their country. If the men hadn't been with us the whole incident would have ended up with awful consequences for us. The whole incident was frightening and seemed to carry the same type of undertones that I'd just been going through in Bursa. I thanked the man for explaining the situation to me and for the way that both men had handled and dealt with it. Yet another nerve racking incident to add to my list that seemed to be endless.

The journey gradually came to an end and we arrived safely at the airport. Both men helped us with our luggage and we said our goodbyes to them and thanked them. They waited until we went through the departure gate to board the plane. I don't know what we'd have done without them on that day.

We passed through the boarding gate to catch our flight to England. I was now seated in the plane as it sped down the runway to take off. At that moment I started having violent pains in my head with the same sensations of being violently clubbed that I'd experienced in the street in Bursa. The pains grew and became intensive and non-stop. I felt that my head was about to split in two. Feeling faint, I pressed the buzzer for the air hostess to bring me a glass of water and told her that I didn't feel well. Then I remembered that I'd packed my bible in my hand luggage and took it out of my bag. I placed it on my head from time to time during the rest of the flight when the pains become too bad.

My actions caused quite a stir with the rest of the passengers when they noticed what I was doing. They must have thought that I was some type of religious fanatic or frightened of flying. Little did they know that I was being attacked by the devil and his demons the whole return flight back to England? On that journey I understood that my ongoing nightmare was far from being over. Another phase of my life was about to begin on my arrival back in England. When we'd landed I was taken off the plane in a wheel chair accompanied by the airhostess as I was too ill to stand up and walk. She'd be wheeling me into the arrivals area. My husband would be waiting for me and was going to have very little sympathy for me or understand the situation and horrors that I'd just been through in Bursa.

Chapter 17

England after Bursa

My husband was at the airport to meet me on arrival at Heathrow when I was pushed into the arrivals area in a wheel chair by the airhostess. Despite feeling exhausted after the journey I noticed right away my husband's distant manner when he came over to me. He greeted me with a few comments about Turkey then asked me briefly what had caused my health condition this time. Then I had to tell him a shortened version of what had taken place in Bursa over the past few months with the supernatural incidents although I knew damn well he didn't believe a word that I was saying. My husband thought that my story was a made up one to cover up what had really been going on in Turkey. I could see this by the look on his face. I told him that my condition was a reoccurrence of the trouble that I'd suffered with since Ankara and that this time it had been a lot worse.

I knew that I was wasting my time telling my husband about my problems. This time around was going to be very difficult for me living at home still being demonized. A few days before arriving in England I'd called a friend and arranged to stay with her for a couple of days before returning home. On mentioning this to my husband he drove me directly to her house from the airport. When my husband dropped me off there I sensed an uncomfortable atmosphere. Linda had agreed for me to stay with her but on my arrival at her house I felt she was already regretting the offer. When we'd arrived I'd gone into the front room to say hello to Linda's husband and while I was doing this Linda and my husband were talking together in whispers in the hall until he left.

After dinner that evening I left the room for something and when I came back Linda and her husband were whispering together but stopped abruptly when I came back into the room. This made me feel very ill at ease being with them. That night when I went to bed I only slept for very brief periods and those were filled with night terrors and bad dreams.

My hopes of peace had been shattered again on the first night that I spent at Linda's house as the demonization of my body hadn't ended. Now I was having the same trouble with another sleepless night. On boarding the flight in Istanbul I thought that the horrors of Bursa were left behind but they weren't, the voices were still with me.

The following morning I felt nervous and edgy at breakfast because I'd been suffering with terrifying ordeals throughout the night and hadn't got much sleep. During breakfast I asked Linda where the nearest church was because I wanted to visit one. She told me there was one not too far away from where she lived and that she'd take me after breakfast. When we'd finished breakfast I showered and dressed quickly then Linda and myself walked down to the church which only took about ten minutes. On our arrival we found the church door open so we went straight in.

On entering the church I noticed how peaceful and calm the atmosphere was with the sunlight streaming through its beautiful stained glass windows that made patterns on the floor. All the windows were covered with stories from the bible with icons of saints and of Jesus Christ and Our Lady. The surrounding walls were of grey stone which gave the church a calm demeanor. Linda sat down on one of the pews as I went directly up to the front of the church to the altar. Linda told me later that I'd knelt down and prayed for some time in front of the altar. Not being very religious herself she thought my lengthy praying was a bit weird. While I was still in front of the alter praying, I suddenly felt a tap on my shoulder and heard Linda saying that we had to go as she had things to do at home. By the way that she spoke to me I gathered that my actions in the church praying made no sense to her.

As we were leaving the church I had a vision of Linda and my husband when I'd arrived at her home. It was of them both remaining in the hall for some time talking in whispers together until he left. It struck me as odd now. What did they have to whisper about for so long? Could he have been telling her something about me and what he thought had taken place in Turkey? These thoughts kept rushing round in my mind as we walked back to her house. I could see that her patience with me was reaching its limit.

When we returned to Linda's house after the visit to the church I felt very uncomfortable and knew that she wanted me out of her house and gone! Throughout that day she kept giving me strange glances and asking me what was the matter with me. My reply was always the same... it was just a health issue bothering me. The condition that I was suffering with was continuing and I knew that Linda wasn't the person to discuss my problems with as she'd never believe me.

On the morning of the second day at her house I woke up ill. I could hardly walk and was deathly white, shivering and about to collapse. When Linda saw me and the condition that I was in she appeared to be somewhat agitated as it was going to cause her more bother. I needed support to walk and I said I needed to see a doctor quickly. Linda agreed with me and her husband drove us to their local hospital's emergency department.

When we arrived at the hospital we waited for a short time and then I was seen by a doctor who immediately asked me if I was a drug user. I replied that I wasn't but the doctor kept repeating to me "you're taking drugs." Then he asked me if I'd just returned from Turkey. My reply was that I had. What had that got to do with how ill I was? By this time I was feeling very traumatized and faint and not helped by the doctor's statements. He continued by stating that all drug addicts deny the fact that they're on drugs. Then he asked me about any symptoms that I'd been experiencing and suffering with since Turkey? I explained briefly some of the symptoms with visions and voices that I'd experienced. Instantaneously I wished I hadn't told him anything as I knew what my information was leading to. His diagnosis required that I should be admitted into hospital immediately for observation and tests.

I replied to the doctor saying that I wasn't staying in the hospital and having any tests done on me because I was not a drug addict and would not be treated like one. When this incident was taking place I was in a consulting room at the hospital with Linda and the doctor. When a sudden great force began to enter my body and I started to feel very light with a floating feeling like I was being lifted up. Then a kind of peace swept over me and I remembered nothing until I found myself standing outside the hospital not knowing how I'd got there. I was still wearing my nightdress, slippers and feeling like I was about to collapse. Linda told me later that I just seemed to disappear from the consulting room. They'd found me standing outside the hospital to everyone's surprise. How I'd got there no one appeared to know, neither did I. Feeling really light headed, all I could hear was Linda's voice sounding very annoyed. It kept repeating "you should have done what the doctor told you and stayed in hospital."

On arrival back at her house, she told me the doctor had given her some medicine for me to take for my problem. She then disappeared into the other room to phone my husband to ask him to come and take me home. Through being demonized I'd now been labelled as a drug addict. Linda had no sympathy for me now. She continued by saying "you've got a child at home, you can't look after him in your condition? Do what the doctor told you and take your medicine." She nearly said 'drug addict' but didn't. There was no going back now. She wanted me out of her house with my drug problems.

Her voice kept echoing in my head non-stop repeating that I should be in hospital to sort myself out, having tests and getting my body clean from what I'd been taking. Her words haunted and hurt me as she believed I was a fully-fledged drug addict who wasn't capable of looking after a young child and that I shouldn't be allowed to be at home with him. She carried on by saying that the doctor had advised her to inform my husband of my problem which she'd already done. The damage was done and the wheels of my fate set in motion when she'd phoned him to take me home. Linda then asked me to pack my things quickly and leave. I agreed that was the best thing to do as I wasn't welcome in her home and I knew that for sure now.

My husband arrived later to take me home and I knew things were not going to get better now being labelled a drug addict. The whole situation was totally ridiculous but I felt like a stranger in my own home. Things were definitely going to get worse from now on compared to previously when I'd returned with the condition a year ago from Ankara. The doctor had prescribed lots of tablets that were for drug addiction which was a misdiagnosis that he never should have made. The medications made me feel chronically ill for the next few weeks with terrible side effects. I had symptoms and feelings of being paralyzed in my legs and other parts of my body. My thoughts were of dying with whatever was living inside my body. I had no one to talk to or confide in at that time about my problem.

For the next few weeks I remained in an oblivious 'phased out' state the whole time. I was living in a strange world that was going on inside my body and head. Flashing images would appeared in front of me whenever I watched TV. They seemed to be linked with whatever was happening to me. This unknown force came into my mind blurring everything out that was real in my existence. The condition became totally alien for me and hard to live with.

The whole atmosphere at home was strange being with my family and husband again. When he spoke to me now it was like he was talking to a stranger that he didn't know. It did upset me a great deal because we'd been married for many years and he should have known that I wasn't lying about what I was going through with this awful condition. Throughout the following weeks I was living in a supernatural world full of confusion. I still kept having crazy thoughts that Tarik had put a hex or curse on me that I'd never recover or survive from. Of course that was all rubbish! Living with this condition puts crazy thoughts into your mind.

The atmosphere at home gradually became tenser as my husband must have thought that I'd been taking drugs with Tarik and that's what had caused my ill health. I'd never used drugs of any type and now I was labelled as being a two timing wife plus a drug addict. My image had changed drastically from being a workaholic in show business to a drug addict. It was hard for me to believe what I was being accused of as my life turned into an apparent scandalous story of sinful sex and drugs with a pending divorce in motion. Since I'd arrived home I'd repeated to my husband several times the full story of what happened when I wasn't in the hotel when he rang. He just continued refusing to accept the truth which I was telling him, helping to destroy our marriage. While all this was taking place, the perpetrators from hell continued causing ongoing troubles with my health.

After I'd been suffering for several weeks I decided to go and see my family doctor. He told my husband that he should have called him earlier for a home visit since my condition wasn't improving. My health by then was in a pretty bad state following my return from Turkey a few weeks earlier. Our family doctor took me off the hospital medication and gave me something else. Changing the medication helped but I was still very lethargic during the day and had to keep lying down and resting.

Before this supernatural trouble took place I'd been a sharp thinking person full of life with a career and a stable family life. On my return home this time I was a dithering lifeless individual lacking energy who was labelled a drug addict. My life had been turned upside down by a gang of demons who'd been doing this since Ankara for the past year. Demonization changed everything in my life from normal to disastrous. Since the hospital doctor's report, everyone seemed to treat me with quite a different attitude, assuming that I must have been taking drugs for some time. The demons used the ongoing situation with treacherous brainwashing, using lies to break up and destroy my marriage. I was still ignorant of the root cause of all my problems.

My husband stuck to his own opinions about my condition and the supernatural things which he never believed were happening to me. When I kept explaining were the cause of my illness. Through misunderstandings between us, everything gradually turned into a chaotic state. After Linda gave my husband the message from the doctor's report, who can blame his reaction towards me? I'd hoped after so many years of being together that he'd know my character and that I'd never be doing drugs of any kind. Once again I was isolated in dealing with my problems. Since my return from Turkey I hadn't contacted my parents to worry them about what had happened to me. I thought my husband might have already mentioned something to them. I found out later he hadn't telephoned or contacted them to say I was at home and not well.

When I phoned my parents they were surprised to hear that I was home and asked why I hadn't I phoned them before. I mentioned that I had been unwell since I'd come home and didn't want to worry them with my problems. After telling my father and mother about my health condition they both did start worrying. I knew this would happen. My father then insisted that I call him every day to let him know how my health was progressing. During the conversation with my father I mentioned quite a bit about what had taken place in Turkey and my health issues that I was suffering with. I also told him that now I was being treated by my family doctor. My father asked me how my husband was keeping and I didn't mention anything to him about our marriage problems.

Shortly after speaking to my parents I bought a magazine about psychics and healers that gave me some hope of finding someone who might be able to help me. Previously I'd seen people from the church who hadn't been able to take away the root cause of my problem which meant I needed to continue looking for an answer to be set free from my nightmare. That's how my endless journey began which has continued on for over half of my lifetime in search of my Holy Grail of deliverance. During those years I visited and met a variety of different people including priests, healers and psychics and many others who all claimed to have some type of answer that could help me. My journey began with making an appointment to see a medium and healer who lived quite a distance away who claimed to have dealt with many cases similar to mine with entities.

During my session with her she said that I did have entities in my body which she thought was a form of possession. In the session she'd removed some entities that she thought must have been with me for some time. After seeing her I returned to regular healing sessions each week for the next few months with hands on healing that made me feel a lot calmer and better in health. I knew that I wasn't completely set free as the voices were still rooted inside my ears and stomach area and still troubled me.

I was in England for quite a while and managed to find a part time job with a promotion company working instore which I did for the next few months. Working kept me active and out of the house three days a week and kept me busy coping with a job. I couldn't recapture my past life at home it had gone although I still loved and cared about my family. My marriage was over due to what I was suffering with. The whole experience was like having a boa constrictor coiled around my private life which was squeezing and destroying everything including my health and career until there was nothing left in my world.

Believe me I know demon strongholds are pure evil that bring affliction and bondage to the body and mind. Over the passing months since Bursa I kept re-living every nightmare of horror, over and over again. I could not erase them from my mind. I tried to put positive thoughts into my mind about the future and my whole situation changing back to a normal life again. With this goal set in my mind, I had something positive to work towards. Being an optimist at heart, I thought my plans would work out and give me a fresh start in my life working again in show business which had always been my career for many years.

Chapter 18

April Fool's Day Istanbul

Eventually I did get another group of dancers together and began rehearsals for a new show. From the first day with this new venture, things started going wrong. To start with, some of the dancers dropped out. Then the music went badly wrong and had to be changed. I began to have my doubts about whether I could cope and organize another show. Preparing one takes a lot of energy and stamina to do the choreography and perform in yourself. While I was rehearsing I continued to experience various symptoms from the demonization which was still haunting my body. My health hadn't fully recovered enough to be working again and travelling abroad with a new show.

Then I had an offer of a contract for Greece which I was about to accept when it was cancelled. It seemed obvious to me now that it wasn't the right time for me to look for work. Everything just kept going wrong. Can anyone who's reading this book guess what comes next? Here it comes... a surprise phone call from Mr. Macy! He said that he could fix a month's contract for the show in Turkey working at a new club that was being renovated in Istanbul. I called the dancers together and informed them about the contract and they all agreed to do it. When I agreed to sign the contract for this job I was still experiencing various symptoms. About a week or so later, the tickets arrived and we left for Istanbul where more horrific supernatural warfare was waiting to engulf me into a web of deception and turmoil.

This chapter of events would be the last one that would take place in Turkey. I took this contract because I couldn't wait forever with my life on hold until this abomination ended. I convinced myself that I could cope and it wouldn't interfere with my work this time. We arrived in Istanbul on April fool's day and as the saying goes "there's no fool like an old fool." We were met at the airport as usual by Mr. Macy who took us straight to a hotel situated in central Istanbul close to the club. Looking back now on Istanbul and all the trauma that took place there, it did turn out to be an April fool's day for me, taking that contract.

After the first day of rehearsals at the club no one seemed to have any idea when the club was opening and this went on for the next two weeks. The club manager kept repeating to me each day that the club would be opening shortly. It became another game of patience waiting to hear when we'd start work. As the days passed by.

Being back in Turkey again, my condition resurfaced with vicious attacks taking place. The intensity of them this time was high, they were filled with evil treachery and cunning against my life. The dormant serpent uncoiled and raised his head again to destroy my health and work once more with the nightly attacks. The sleep deprivation set in again night after night, dragging me down into a vortex of hellish situations. What I'd dreaded had resurfaced again and uprooted all my memories from the past year as things turned gradually into another type of Bursa experience that cast a dark shadow of oppression over my body and into mind. When I'd left England I knew that I was taking a chance working abroad again with a new show, still suffering with my ongoing condition.

It was twelve days now since we'd arrived in Istanbul and still there were no signs of the club opening. The renovation and repairs were still going on while we continued rehearsing at the club over the next two weeks hoping there was going to be an opening night soon. I was beginning to have my doubts about the contract and the risk that I'd taken coming to Istanbul. Whenever I spoke to the manager about the opening day he'd smile and say just a few more days. Although I wanted to believe him I kept having the feeling that I was heading for another disaster by taking this contract. The money that I brought with me from England was running out rapidly now and at the point where we needed to start work.

My days in Istanbul were an ongoing battle to survive with my health and the insecurity of not knowing when we'd be starting work. From my own past experience of living with demons, I know that they can ruin a person's life through their attacks. Once they're in motion in a body they can drive a sane person nuts over time. When they attempt to corrupt a victim. If it doesn't work, the next step is to destroy or kill a person through illness or suicide. Believe me I know what I'm talking about. Don't ever play around with demonic strongholds. They're trained assassins ready and waiting for combat against the human race. Always be vigilant as the enemy is waiting to trap people and enter their lives to destroy them.

I return back to my story. We did finally start work at the club but then more weird and macabre incidents began taking place nightly. One evening after the first show I began to feel quite ill so I couldn't remain to do the second part and had to return to the hotel. Through this same situation of ongoing health problems taking place a couple of times I lost my salary. The show continued working at the club without me for a few days. I hoped that I'd be well enough to go back to work and things would settle down. Istanbul wasn't going to be an easy period for me.

There were many repeating scenarios from the past that started ruining my work with the show again. This time they were more intense with a greater force of evil intent on destroying me. I continued persevering every day to do my job. I was tense and tired at that time and finding it hard to cope again.

Then the dancers in my show appeared to be very unsettled and whispered amongst themselves all the time. It was clear to me now that the show was on the verge of breaking up. There were a multitude of warning signs on the horizon for myself and the show. During that time as things got worse, I thought that some type of magic was being conjured up as revenge against me and that Tarik was doing it. This was totally ridiculous as his time was always spent thinking about his job. I found myself asking the same question over and over again… who else could be doing these terrible things to me non-stop?

In the meantime the situation at the club became very unsettled with numerous incidents taking place. It started with our costumes from the show being thrown on the floor after we'd hung them up neatly, then things that we used in the show went missing and couldn't be found. Gradually over the passing days our work at the club was turning into a catastrophe along with my health.

On another night at the club my shoes that I use in the show were broken and the pads taken out of my costumes. Other items that we used in the show became misplaced or torn after we'd put all our costumes away in the changing room the previous night in good condition before leaving the club. While these disturbances continued taking place at the club nightly, I was suffering attacks on my body which were getting worse and harder for me to handle emotionally. The dizzy spells returned and the lack of energy resulted in further deterioration of my body.

The torments with the attacks now included violent undertones of memories from the past year with visions of Tarik in Ankara. They turned into nightmares and then visions of my family and Bursa which wouldn't stop haunting me if I slept in the hotel. Once again I began having terrible pains in my head like needles being dug into my scalp and pricking sensations moving around in my stomach and entire body. The perpetrators from hell would stop at nothing to ruin my health and my chances of success.

With all this ongoing friction and stress in Istanbul I didn't know if I'd be strong enough to carry on working. How could I prove to anyone that this phenomenon was really happening to me as it couldn't be seen visually? Another incident took place at the hotel when I was told that I couldn't phone England. I had to go to the Hilton Hotel to make a call home. After doing this I changed hotel with my group to see if things would improve and quiet down. They didn't! Things just got worse as the supernatural force carried on battering and destroying everything for me. Being deprived of sleep at night was causing drastic effects on my health living with this endless prison sentence of horrors. Our working conditions at the club had now grown unbearable. My dancers never stopped complaining about the work at the club which didn't help matters as I was feeling chronically ill at this time.

Then one afternoon when I left the hotel to get a few things done and phone home, I suddenly started having terrible gripping pains in my entire body and stomach area in the street. The sensations I felt were like being violently punched in the stomach as the pain exploded into my abdomen. Every time this took place I doubled up in pain. Feeling very ill, in I returned to the hotel and took some tablets for the pain and had to rest for the afternoon until the pain eased. After that day the stomach pains occurred frequently at various times. How could I mention what was happening to me again to any of my group?

During that time everything at the club was still going wrong and then the dancers told me that they wanted to break their contracts and return to England. Once again I was in jeopardy of losing everything through suffering with this condition. Desperately needing advice I decided to see the consul in Istanbul. I went ahead and did this. On seeing him, I enquired at the same time about an appointment to see the priest who took Sunday mass. I saw the priest a few days later who was very helpful and gave me some information on what he thought I might be suffering with. He discussed my condition with me at length and I found it quite difficult explaining everything that had happened to me since it began in Ankara. The priest seemed to have quite a bit of knowledge on the type of supernatural condition that I had and advised me to see a priest who was experienced in dealing with these type of cases once I returned to England.

Over the next few nights the working conditions at the club grew worse and I had to nag the club for our salary each night. The manager didn't want to pay what he'd agreed to originally in the contract. With so many unsettling things going on, I still tried to find a solution to continue and finish the contract. We didn't! There was no way to resolve the problems that kept arising with the club. I'd reached breaking point again as there were too many different issues going on at that time. I just couldn't take any more mental pressure with the situation in Istanbul. That is why I took the decision to end the whole thing and broke the contract with the club and arranged to leave Turkey.

When the day of departure came around I was fleeing Istanbul with a repeat performance of that from Bursa with the devils at my heels. It reminded me of the song **Hit the Road Jack...** and don't you come back no more, no more, no more. This could have been written for me as my theme tune. The taxis arrived at the hotel and we left for Istanbul airport with me running short of money. I didn't have enough money to pay for all the excess baggage of the costume trunks so I had to leave a lot of stuff behind in order to get out of Turkey. Since my departure from Turkey during the 1980s I've never returned there.

Chapter 19

Various Supernatural Incidents

On my return to England from Turkey I had to have an operation which was caused by the attacks in Istanbul. They had made a large fibroid develop which was attached to my womb. After seeing a doctor, I had to have an emergency hysterectomy operation so the fibroid and womb could both be removed. I didn't realize at the time what was still inside my body and going to cause more damage and ongoing infirmities over the coming years.

Having this condition inside my body would become more dangerous the longer it remained inside me. After my operation, I took the advice that I'd been given by the priest in Istanbul and phoned the church to see what was required to become confirmed into the Church of England. After receiving all the information I went ahead and attended classes for some time to learn more about the church. Then I was confirmed in the September at Marylebone Parish Church. By being confirmed into the church I thought that gradually it would help set me free from the horrific ordeal which has continued to cling onto my body.

After Ankara

Nailed to the Cross Horror

When I returned from Ankara the first time when the issues began I went to see a doctor. He recommended that a nurse from the hospital would come to my home to inject me with a heavy sedative which would help relieve the condition which I was suffering from and experiencing. The nurse came and injected me with some medication that put me out for a few days. During that time I was in a traumatic state not knowing what was happening to me. I was totally comatose and in a 'phased out' state lost in a strange world of pain with non-stop whispering voices still with me.

Something strange had happened to my body and the whole life that I'd had. My family life and career all seemed to have disappeared along with my health. I was in a totally oblivious state for a month or so and couldn't speak to anyone about what I was experiencing. As the whispering voices became more threatening and abusive towards me daily. Then to top it all I might have ended up in a mental hospital as well if I hadn't stood my ground. This is an example of what this horrific condition can create in a person's life once it enters a victim's body.

During this period while I was living at home with my family, my health steadily grew worse. Brainwashing accompanied the bombardment of lies coming from the voices with the attacks. Then one afternoon when I was lying down trying to rest on the couch in the back room of my house, the voices told me that I was going to be sacrificed otherwise my husband and son were going to suffer. Telepathically I agreed to anything so that the demonic stronghold wouldn't hurt or attack my family. Then the voices told me that this was an act sent from God. By that time the demonic stronghold knew that I wouldn't want to disobey God so they used this tactic to instil acts of fear and obedience in me.

What took place next was horrifying. All of a sudden I began to feel excruciating pain as if nails were being hammered into me. When this was happening I began screaming and my husband must have thought that I was totally mad because he got a cross and held it up in front of me! The couch that I was lying on began to shake violently under me as I had the sensation of being crucified. While this was taking place a raging storm with heavy rain and thunder was going on outside. With the rain beating against the windows of the back room that I was in. Suddenly the cross that my husband was holding cracked in half and a panel of the door split... it was all very extraordinary. I was still lying dazed on the couch when I saw a vision of a pair of feet that were nailed to a cross bleeding into a pool of water that I think was rain. The key weapons the demons used with their spiritual warfare against me were God and religion.

The next couple of years passed by quickly with ongoing tormenting attacks continuing that caused me to have another operation through the ongoing damage being done to my inside. I was unable to discuss the real root of my problem with my doctor and what I was suffering with inside my body. This time the attacks had caused me to lose control of my water works. Eventually I made an appointment to see my doctor and he told me what I already suspected that I needed another operation for a bladder repair. I went ahead and had it done. This operation took me a lengthy time to recover from as while the healing process was taking place I was still being attacked daily.

Switzerland during the 1990s

In the 1990s I attempted to work again with my shows and got a three month contract to work in Switzerland. Although I was still suffering with effects of my ongoing condition I managed to work through a couple of the contract successfully. Then towards the end of the last month's contract things started repeating themselves to a higher degree with the demonization so I was forced once again to finish the contract early with the club where I was working before my condition became unmanageable for me to handle. I started making the arrangements for the show to leave Switzerland.

On this particular afternoon I decided to go into Zurich which was quite near to where we were working with the dancers to spend a leisurely afternoon of sightseeing. I planned to phone my agent who was also in Zurich while we were there to let him know how the arrangements were going for us to leave. This way everything could be done in advance for my show to finish the contract and travel a couple of days later back to England.

My plan was to discuss everything with the agent while I was in Zurich that afternoon. Little did I know what was about to take place on that lovely sunny afternoon. Out of the blue that afternoon all of us would experience and be involved in a paranormal manifestation which took place inside a phone booth. When we arrived in Zurich I decided to phone the agent straight away so we'd have the rest of the afternoon free to look around.

I found a phone booth reasonably quickly, opened the door and went inside with a couple of the girls. The rest of them were standing outside. Then I dialed the agent's phone number. He answered and I started telling him about the arrangements that I'd made for the show to finish at the club. In the middle of our conversation a slight tremor began taking place inside the phone booth, then suddenly the booth began to shake violently. While it was shaking phone books fell off the shelf onto the floor. Next they began flying around us and hitting the sides of the booth. While this was taking place the agent's voice began to grow fainter on the phone until I couldn't hear him at all. Suddenly the line went dead and he was cut off completely.

By this time the girls who were with me were screaming and shouting hysterically. The three of us tried to push the door of the booth open to get out. We tried several times without success... the door wouldn't open. Now the girls with me were crying and shouting asking me what was happening. Like I'm supposed to know what's going on? The girls who were in the street started pushing the door from the other side but the door still wouldn't budge. Everyone was frightened now by the manifestation that we were all witnessing and part of. We all continued pushing the door with as much force as we could, then suddenly the shaking began to slow down in the booth. The door of the phone booth swung open with a loud screeching sound that filled the air and we got out!

When we were out of the phone booth we all just clung to each other for several minutes in the street finding comfort in being free in the fresh air after the terrifying ordeal we'd just been through locked in the phone booth. It certainly was a close encounter with the forces of evil that had materialized out of nowhere that day. I made no other attempts to phone the agent but did it when we returned to our hotel. These types of incidents make you more aware of how nerve racking and disturbing these paranormal encounters are for other people and not just myself living with them constantly.

The Zurich incident frightened and affected my group who now did believe what I'd told them previously about my experiences with the supernatural. Now they'd seen a weird and strange phenomenon in action and it had terrified them. After the manifestation I realized that the powers and principalities of wickedness were still close to me wherever I went. The manifestation in the booth had left its stigma of fear in the group and all my dancers wanted to leave Switzerland as quickly as possible.

Another close encounter in Italy

I was working in Italy this time when an accident we had could have caused the death of us all to take place. It happened on the way back to our hotel after work one night in the early hours of the morning. The contract I had this time was at a club which was several miles away from where we lived. Every night after work we'd be driven back to our hotel in Vercelli by one of the waiters who worked at the club. On this particular night the person who usually drove us back was busy still clearing up at the club and couldn't take us. One of my dancers who had an international driving license said that she'd drive us back to the hotel. That night I got into the car with my handbag and a bundle of costumes that needed washing and climbed into the back seat of the car. Once I was seated the other people piled into the car until it was packed with seven or eight of us.

Once the car doors were slammed shut we began our journey back to Vercelli to our hotel. On leaving the club behind in the distance I kept praying that we didn't have an accident because there were too many people in the car. The road we were on was clear as it was in the early hours of the morning. Everyone in the car was tired after a long night at the club but that didn't stop the usual few girls singing along with the latest pop music that blared out from the radio. If the girls weren't singing they'd be chatting together non-stop for the rest of the journey back to the hotel.

That night was going to be different after the car took a sharp bend around a corner and hit something in the road. The impact of what was hit made the car go completely out of control and head towards the river which lay straight ahead of us. The girl who was driving the car began to panic and lost control of herself. She knew the situation was a dangerous one and the car wouldn't stop and was heading directly towards the water's edge where the road ended. The car couldn't be stopped and went half way over the edge and then suddenly came to a halt. We just hung there! The car was hanging half way over the water. The girl who was driving the car was unable to do anything as it was off the ground and hanging in midair. We were in a very dangerous position now because if anyone made an attempt to climb out of the car or open the doors it could overbalance and go straight into the water which was deep and flowing downstream very fast.

Finding help at that time of the morning was going to be hard. We were in the countryside and on a very desolate road that very few people took. There was silence in the car now and everyone must have been praying to God for help. I certainly was! The owner of the car was a Buddhist and kept repeating that Buddha would sort the situation out. Well the more the merrier... we needed whatever help we could get to survive the situation were in. The atmosphere in the car was tense as everyone was frightened to move in case it tipped forward and we'd all end up being drowned in the water below us. The water was an uninviting muddy dark brown color.

I was sitting in the back of the car squeezed tightly in-between two of my dancers where the two back wheels of the car were just on the edge of the ground. The slightest movement would have sent us rolling forward into the water. My premonition on that night about an accident through the car being overloaded with people and had turned into reality now. We were in a very dangerous situation... if the car rolled forward there would be a major accident. How could we get help? It looked impossible at that moment in time. The car needed to be pulled back onto the road and this needed to be done by another car with ropes attached to our car. The situation looked bad and to top it all we were stuck in the middle of the countryside, we'd taken a short cut that night going back to Vercelli as it was quicker. Very few people took this route so I began to wonder if anyone would find us on this road. Maybe some of the waiters would find us going home from the club? These types of thoughts kept going round in my mind as I sat silent and afraid to move.

Then suddenly out of nowhere a man came into sight who must have parked his car somewhere else. He came walking towards us with his fishing tackle and came over and spoke to us the best he could shouting and doing sign language. I don't remember exactly what took place but he offered to go back to the club to get help for us which he did. Within a short space of time the man arrived back with some of the waiters from the club. They did exactly what I thought and put ropes onto the back of the car then gradually pulled it back upright onto the ground and then towed it very slowly back onto the road.

Everyone in the car was badly shaken by the ordeal that we'd all just been through, especially the girl who'd been driving the car that night. She was shaking and still in shock and unable to drive anymore that night. The Buddhist drove us back to the hotel claiming as she drove that her God had saved us all. She showed us all a statue of Buddha that she'd hidden behind a glove cupboard in the front of the car. I'd never noticed or seen it until that night. We were all safe through another strange miracle that had just taken place against all odds. Thank you God!

Healer Nightmare Visit 2012

In 2012 I made an appointment to see a healer who'd been recommended to me by some people who had seen him with their children. I thought automatically that if a family take their children to see this person it must be safe to visit him.

I was thinking that the appointment with this healer might be of some help as I was still suffering a lot with my ongoing condition which I still hadn't got rid of. If the first visit went ok I could start seeing the healer on a regular basis. When I arrived for the appointment I was told to sit in a waiting room until it was my turn to be seen. The waiting room was quite small and full of people and there was a very powerful-smelling incense being burned that filled the air. Eventually my turn came around and I was ushered into another small room and told to make myself comfortable. To be truthful, I felt very uneasy and nervous about where I was. I'd never experienced this sensation before when visiting other healers. I can't explain what it was. The whole place had a strange atmosphere

All of a sudden there was a noise outside the room that I was waiting in. The door then swung open and a tall fair man walked in dressed in an orange robe. Straight away he spoke to me in a very aggressive manner. He asked me a question. ''Why did you go and get these things get inside your body?'' I tried to explain my problem and condition to him and why I'd come to see him but he just didn't want to listen. By this time I was feeling very nervous and ill at ease with him. Then he repeated the same question to me several times. "Why did you go and get these things get inside your body?" Then without any warning he opened my trouser zip and put something on my solar plexus. I asked him what he was doing. I felt shocked by his actions. He didn't reply but pressed down on my abdomen with a great pressure that felt like a bolt of lightning had gone through my stomach. When he did this I started having violent chest pains and started to collapse. I felt as though I'd just had an operation. He stated "you have!"

Feeling sick now and giddy with ongoing chest pains I needed to lie down. While I was in this state the so called healer continued shouting at me and then slapped me around the face. He then told one of his assistants to throw water over me just as I was collapsing. When I mentioned that I needed to go to a hospital I was ignored. Then two people who work with him came into the room to help hold me up as I couldn't stand up. I repeated several times that I needed to go to a hospital and was ignored.

I could have died in that place with that so called healer's treatment. This man had no compassion or interest in any after-care or in what he'd just done to me. He had left me so ill but he didn't care. Being really traumatized I kept asking for a taxi to go to hospital as I had a pain shooting down my arm. I had a bad hiatus hernia and feared that it could trigger a heart attack. Then I felt the room going round and collapsed. I was feeling like I was about to die as the pain grew worse. All I could hear in that shocked state was the healer's voice from hell still shouting at me. Then he ordered two of his helpers to get me out of that room as he had other people to see. They put me into the waiting room on a chair with my belongings thrown under the chair and left me there in a shocked dazed state, lying across the chair.

Nobody in the waiting room came over to help me. They just stared at me but did nothing. Lying on the chair, I gradually lost track of time. I stayed there for quite a while as I still couldn't stand up on my own. Who cared about me in that place? No-one! During this period of time the demonic spirits inside me were paralyzing my arms and legs and shaking me at the same time. God, what had I done to deserve this horrific condition?

Finally, I forced myself to get up and put on my boots and gather up my things together so I could leave. I asked for a mini cab to take me to the station. How was I going to get back home in this condition being all alone? When the cab arrived I could still hardly walk because of the horrifying experience I'd just been through with the healer from hell. With great difficulty, I managed to catch my train home with people looking at me all the time. I was shaking and deathly white but still alive. What a relief as the train pulled out of the station! I'd managed to get away from the chamber of horrors that I'd visited that day.

I had to face yet another trial to get home because I needed to get a mini cab from the station. On arriving home I was totally alone in the house as my son was still in America and coming home the next day. The rest of the day was spent lying down in my bedroom not knowing how I'd survived that horrendous attack. The gang of demons must have been puzzled and wondering why the healer's attempt to kill me hadn't worked. I'd survived again another ongoing attack while living with my ordeal. My survival allows me to be able to tell my story of what demonization can do to a person's life.

During the 1990s I managed further groups and worked in Belgium with a Greek family-run club. I then worked with my dance shows for a few months in Israel, Italy, Greece and Holland. After the 1990s, my show business life gradually came to an end and I had to close the doors on it.

Chapter 20

1990s to 2004

Another chapter began in my life during the 1990s that took me on a journey doing in-store promotion work which I continued doing up to 2004. During those years, I worked in most of the major stores and supermarkets around central London and the Essex area. I worked with various agencies in different stores promoting whatever products I was given each week.

Then I started a three year part time college course learning about counselling. I continued studying and went on to learn about hypnosis which I thought might help me with the condition I was suffering with. Despite still being affected by demonization during those three years, I managed to complete the courses and gained both of the certificates.

With my ongoing battle of being demonized still going on inside my body, the task of holding onto my full time manager's job in a charity shop was a hard one to maintain. Keeping this job helped to pay for my college courses. Throughout those years I never stopped searching for answers to end my suffering living with my endless condition. I thought that by the time I'd completed my exams I'd be free from my condition having found the answer. I'd start my own practice as a hypnotherapist by year 2000 when my exams finished.

The plan that I had once I'd passed my exams was to work from home as a practicing hypnotherapist never materialized because new people moved in next door with a lot of children. They started converting the property with construction work and doing repairs that went on for several years. After spending quite a lot of money on my college courses, my dream of starting a practice was put on hold and then faded into the blue.

My struggle to survive still suffering with the condition continued. In 2001 I became a permanent demonstrator for a supermarket and remained working there until June 2004 when the store changed management. During that time I was continuously visiting doctors and hospitals with different health issues.

From 2004 onwards a lot of my time was spent with my father at his home as he needed help with his everyday needs. The ageing process was taking its toll on his life causing a gradual deterioration of his health. I was spending quite a few days of each week going in-between his home and mine. On top of this I also had to find time to visit my Down's syndrome sister Valerie who was in a nursing home.

Throughout this period I was becoming frailer myself due to living with the demonization as I got nearer to retirement. Once my permanent job ended I never stopped worrying about how I was going to survive and pay the bills if I couldn't find another job.

During this time I never mentioned to my father that I was still suffering with nightly demonic attacks. Which had remained with me draining my life away up to 2017. While I was thinking about what I could do to get a job, an idea came to me. I could start doing some singing again and look for singing jobs at nursing homes and ladies clubs where they use entertainers for special occasions. These jobs are few and far between and difficult to get until you get yourself known. Thinking this was a good idea, I phoned and wrote off to a few different places. I did get some bookings doing one-hour sing-alongs in nursing homes and ladies clubs which went down well with the audiences.

I enjoyed doing these jobs and would have continued with them if my health had been better. Doing these venues meant that I had to assemble all the amplification equipment for the gig and then pack up everything at the end of my show myself. I also had to arrange transport to get home. With the non-stop attacks still going on and voices trying to drive me insane (especially when I was concentrating on a task), they were difficult times for me. I had to remember a lot of words from the songs and keep the audience entertained which was difficult while being abused physically and mentally. Living with this condition has been a life threatening and nerve racking experience for me to bare.

Living with a demonic stronghold out to destroy everything you attempt to do in your life is awful. If I hadn't been suffering with this horrific condition I could have coped with the singing jobs and looked for more work doing these types of venues full time.

In 2005 another tragedy struck when my younger Down's syndrome sister Valerie died in that December. Up to that time I'd been seeing my sister on a regular basis and acting as a go-between to assist all her needs. Previously she'd been living in a care home close to where I live for quite a few years and been happy there. Then she'd been moved to another care home which proved to be very traumatic for her. When I visited her at the new home she was generally alone and crying in her bedroom. It really worried me a great deal that she was so unhappy. My sister loved music so I got her a radio and asked the careers to put it on for her when she was left alone in her room.

During this time I was still suffering myself daily. Now I was worrying about her as well because she couldn't speak much to tell you if something or someone was harming her. On the morning when I was given the news that my sister had died, I went into a completely shocked state as I'd been with her the day before on a visit. Why hadn't anyone mentioned to me that she hadn't been well? After her death I was told that she'd been suffering with heart trouble which I'd never been informed about. Many Down's syndrome people often suffer with this condition.

About a month before my sister's death my father also had to go into a care home. It was nearly next door to the one that my sister was in. During that short period many drastic changes took place rapidly in my father's health after I explained to my father that my sister had died. He could never except the fact and constantly reminded me to make sure to go and visit her. He'd always been a vigorous person and a great optimist by nature which made me feel very sad when I saw the decline in him in the care home. It seemed to destroy who he was as an active-minded person who'd always looked after himself. Since my mother died and my sister had gone into care he'd lead a normal life and spent a great deal of time with me at my home.

Eventually my father agreed to go into a care home to be looked after which I regret. While he was still in his own home he remained ok and active but after he moved into the care home he lost his vigorous ways having been labelled as an old person who just needed to sleep and be quiet. Older people have all had lives and families they can talk about with others.

Whenever I visited my father I noticed he was gradually slipping away into a world of sleeping non-stop as there was nothing to keep him interested in life anymore. Once these signs start taking place a person is entering a very dangerous stage of their life and death follows quickly. Care homes are busy but to let older people sleep non-stop isn't the answer in my eyes to help them, it's so they don't bother the staff. Seeing this taking place with my father was another worry for me to dwell on.

Throughout this time I was still living daily with the residents from hell and living in constant turmoil which I never mentioned to my father. My father had always been my guiding light and seeing him going downhill was another issue that I found hard to cope with. Every Sunday he'd come home to me for the day and go back to the care home in the evening to keep some aspect of normality in his world. I visited him as much as I could and kept him updated with news. Visiting my father and my sister while she was alive left me with very little spare time for myself.

Over the passing years as I've grown older my life has remained in constant jeopardy with the spiritual warfare in my body continuing with the abomination. By writing this book I hope the reader appreciates that I've come out of the closet to explain what it's like living with this terrible infliction going on inside your body. Normally this type of subject is not discussed in public or by the people who've suffered with it as the victim will be categorized in an unpleasant group and it carries a stigma. It is only really accepted in horror movies or on TV where the abomination ends after which you can go home and forget about it.

Living with the horror of this experience is something that I can't forget because it's living inside my own body. This is a true story that happened to me which engulfed my whole existence. The only person who actually helped and believed what was happening to me and gave me a positive optimistic outlook to help deal with it was my father. He defended me against all odds. When he died from an infection in hospital in 2006 it was my greatest loss. He was my best friend and father that I had the honor of having in my life who'll always be remembered and missed a great deal.

Chapter 21

Becoming a Catholic

In 2006 I visited my local Catholic shop to buy some candles and a few items. I'd been doing this for years and while I was in the shop I got chatting to the owner. For some unknown reason I started telling her about my long term problem with my condition. She seemed quite interested in my story and told me that she knew a priest who might be able to help me. Then she asked me if I'd like to meet him as she could arrange an appointment for him to see me. I replied by saying that I would be interested in seeing him. She wrote to the priest and I had an answer about a month later saying that he'd see me. The next thing that I needed to do was write a letter to him with the full details of what I'd been suffering with and a little about my background. I did this in a long letter and I posted it off to the priest.

I believed at that time my prayers were finally being answered and that my nightmare was gradually going to come to an end through the power of God and I'd be set free. About a week later I received a reply to my letter asking me to phone the priest for an appointment and I began visiting him in 2006. The sessions continued over the next four years. My first appointment consisted of an interview with many personal questions about my life, faith and also about what measures I'd taken to rid myself of the condition. There was another Catholic gentlemen present at the interview with the priest who also asked me some questions about my faith and beliefs. I was feeling confident after the session that I was finally on the right path to be set free.

Previously I had attended the Catholic Church a great deal because my husband and son were Catholics although I'd remained with the Church of England myself. After seeing the priest I began attending mass at Catholic Church on Sundays. I began to learn more about the faith becoming more familiar with its traditions. If I was going to become a Catholic anticipating that I'd eventually find my deliverance through gaining more faith in Christ Jesus. I hoped that I'd taken the right decision in becoming a Catholic and would remain with the church for the rest of my days.

My sessions with the priest consisted of prayer and a form of exorcism that was suitable for my type of condition. The priest that I saw made every effort to alleviate the condition and remove it from my body. The demonization remained clinging onto my body like a leech, draining my life away. I never lost my belief and faith in the power of God to finally remove my condition. In the New Testament we read many stories of Jesus casting out unclean spirits during his ministry on Earth and I believed it would happen for me.

However, I remained puzzled at why I wasn't being delivered after four years of prayers and exorcism. I'd been blessed countless times with holy oil and holy water plus I'd never stopped praying for years to be delivered from the abomination in my body. On entering the Catholic Church I firmly believed that eventually I'd be set free but my deliverance didn't take place during the time that I was with the Catholic Church.

During those years I went on many pilgrimages to shrines and had many visions from 2006 onwards. Being human, all I wanted was a solution to end the issue that I've been suffering with and possibly a miracle. Shrines bring hope for pilgrims who visit them that healings and miracles might take place which keeps a hope factor going for most people. Our lives may be changed forever through God's saving power, Our Lady or through Saints when healings or miracles take place. People are drawn to visit holy places and shrines when they are experiencing great difficulties in their lives or suffering with health issues. Shrines become a quest to visit for people with illness who are always searching for an answer so they can be healed.

I sometimes need assurance from God that he exists and that he hears our prayers. Maybe I read an article in a magazine or paper about someone who's had a miracle recently. I now become interested and wonder where that shrine is and start to feel like I must visit it. The hope factor is back. I'll go there this summer. Miracles are discussed and investigated through documentaries and on TV programs all the time. I'm still waiting for mine and it's turned into a mystery for me why nothing has happened. In reality there's no answer to this question. Maybe I'll be healed on my next visit to a shrine, who knows! We're all in search of our own Holy Grail to find the unobtainable cure and answers so we keep searching for God's almighty power to solve our problems. I have done this on my journey through most of my life.

When a case looks hopeless we remember God and begin to pray for his divine intervention to take place as its Gods turn to help us now. Who else do we have left to call on for help? Let's have a look at the bible. Yes, it says Jesus heals and cures the sick. Yes, the gospels are full of miracles happening and Jesus can do all these wonderful things, so my troubles are over. I'll get in touch with Jesus as my lives in constant jeopardy with no deliverance and I've prayed constantly for years asking for healing and to be set free and delivered.

Here comes the down side! The whole Christian world is on the same phone line to Jesus and God along with the Saints plus the Holy Mother praying fervently for help as I am. You'll have to wait your turn in the queue and at you're at the back of the line. The years pass by and you continue waiting in the queue and praying. Sometimes unexpected things do turn up but not what you're praying for. Yes, I've waited for endless years wondering if God hears my prayers as I've never stopped them since my trouble started. It has been a tremendously long wait for well over thirty years.

Returning to my story, I still believe today that many of the visions which I saw were genuine and did take place. Some of the things I experienced did appear to be signs and intervention coming from God. I'm a natural sensitive and medium so I have the gift of being able to see the visions when they started taking place in Ankara. When my experiences began I was very vulnerable and did not know what was happening to me. It took a long time until I understood my situation and what I was living with.

Jesus of Prague Speaks

After joining the Catholic Church I had quite a few more unusual encounters including one with a little statue of Jesus of Prague when he spoke to me for the first time. It took place while I was working in the kitchen preparing the evening meal. I was surprised when I heard a voice say "No one is perfect." It was even stranger because I'd mended the statue's head that day. A lady in the Catholic Church had given me the statue as a gift. It wasn't a new statue, it had been hers. When she gave me the statue in a bag the head was already off and I mended it with glue.

This incident is completely true. The statue spoke to me and did so quite frequently after that first time. Whenever I made an attempt to speak to the little Jesus statue it would respond by surrounding itself with light while we spoke together. The Jesus statue always told me "not to be afraid" when the eyes and mouth moved or when an arm lifted up to bless me. The little statue of Jesus always seemed to want to talk endlessly with me about his plans for the world. I found the whole experience extraordinary and hard to believe although it was taking place in front of me with the little Jesus statue still talking away to me. We did get on very well like friends and I enjoyed our chats together which gradually became quite frequent.

During that time with Christmas drawing near the Jesus statue asked me to make some clothes, which I did. I made three different sets of clothes in red, white and purple with elaborate tasteful decorations which he seemed to like. One of the set was worn in church that Christmas. I asked the priest if the statue could be placed in the Church over the Christmas period. The Church wasn't too keen on the idea but he went in surrounded by flowers. It remained there for roughly a month. The children liked the Jesus statue but the Church thought that the statue was getting too much attention and didn't want to accept him the following Christmas.

During that time I continued to be battered daily even more while the statue remained in the Church. Throughout this time all sorts of perverted images were being shown to me in visions including ones of Jesus as a grown man. All these perversions were being done by the demonic stronghold. This period was horrific for me and I had to guard my mind carefully and question everything that I saw. From then onwards I began to analyze everything that I experienced to deduct for myself if it was true or not regarding everything that came into my thoughts or visions I had. I've been told several times by religious people that God will remove my demonization in his own time. Where does that leave me today still suffering? I believe Jesus would have removed the condition from my body with just a few words because he had the power to do it.

I've spent half of my life time living with this hellish condition which I'm still suffering with up to the present time. Over the years most people have repeat to me to keep praying and I've never stopped. They really don't understand what it's like living and suffering when you're demonized. I spend most of my nights unable to sleep in peace because I'm being tormented. It devours my immune system and makes me physically weak. Being demonized can cause a victim to become terminally ill through the ongoing 'slaughter' that's being applied to the inside of the body. I don't want to go on living the rest of the years that I have left with this hellish state of abuse going on in my body with no respite.

I continue battling daily with this disastrous condition that's attacking me from the crown of my head to the soles of my feet causing internal bleeding and pain in different parts of my body. I emphasize that this is a very serious condition for any person to suffer with and not a fantasy… it's real. Very few people will ever understand if you talk to them about it. Feeling very low because of not getting deliverance I decided to search for help with other methods to remove the demonic spirits. This is why I returned to the Church of England as they're slightly more open-minded in their views.

When people are suffering with either demonization or possession it's generally kept private and away from the public. People who have either of these conditions need to be dealt with and treated in a proper manner. They both can have similar symptoms to mental illness which is caused by the demonic spirits. When these parasites enter the body and are living in it they cause a great deal of physical and mental issues to accrue. The medical profession fails to recognize this when confronted with a victim who's suffering with either of these conditions.

Many psychiatric doctors do not recognize that the condition exists which leaves people who are suffering with it unable to discuss their problem openly. If the victim does speak about his or her condition they might end up in a mental institute being treated for schizophrenia through misdiagnosis. This issue can bring many hardships for victims to deal with. Before demonization was unleashed into my life I was a fit person with reasonably good health. This condition is a shattering experience for anyone to handle and live with in their everyday life without going insane. You're fighting against all odds every day to survive and keep your mind and body intact.

The attacks have caused a lot of damage that's badly affected my bodily functions. Over the passing years I've remained focused and steadfast, fighting daily against the wiles of the demonic gang who've been aiming to destroy me. Don't ask me how I feel! The condition is an unbearable one to live with. I've existed with it for over thirty four years. I am left still searching for my Holy Grail of deliverance. It's been an ongoing nightmare from the pits of hell for me… and I've been unable to wake up from it.

Chapter 22

Filming the Documentary

In 2010 a lady I'd known for several years who'd worked for me previously in show business was now making documentary films. When we met one day she suggested that the story about my condition would make an interesting documentary film because it was a true story. She already knew that I'd been living with the condition for a number of years and asked me if I'd like to make a documentary about it. I agreed to a film of my story being made. I thought the documentary might help other people who could be suffering with similar symptoms from this condition.

By telling my story it would inform the public that this type of condition is a real one that exists and is still taking place in the society we live in. After I agreed to do the documentary, filming started a few months later. The documentary was about my life in show business and the experiences of how my life changed once I became a victim of demonization after it entered my body in Ankara during the 1980s.

We were hoping that the documentary would be bought by one of the TV Company's and be aired to the public so it could help other people who might be suffering in silence with the condition. Perhaps I could then start up a help group because I know for a fact that people are generally frightened to speak about the condition when it happens to them. I thought that coming out of the closet with my own experiences via the documentary would make people more aware that this type of condition is still taking place in many people's lives who are too afraid to reveal what is happening to them. When demonization enters the human body it becomes equivalent to any other long term illness and needs treatment until the victim is set free from it. This condition leaves behind long lasting mental and physical effects that remain with the victim.

The filming of the documentary continued over the next few years until it was finally finished. Then in 2017, a cut version of the documentary was shown at the Festival of Horror at Southend on Sea and was well-received by the public.

I've lived with this condition up to the present time with its soul-destroying effects inside my body. How can I explain what it feels like being abused physically and mentally around the clock by a gang of demons living inside your own body? That's why victims of these types of conditions really need specialized help for them to survive this horrendous ordeal and get their lives back on track. It requires people who are dedicated and have the knowledge to deal with these types of issues. The right help is needed until deliverance takes place and a person is set free. This is a very dangerous condition for any person to suffer with.

I know about the dangers because I've lived for so many years being oppressed by its bondage. I can confirm that it has affected and damaged my health and left me unable to plan too far ahead with my life. I need to go just from day to day. My life is being held in constant jeopardy through the overwhelming trauma and stress of having to cope with this daily situation. As I've grown older and frailer still having these attacks non-stop has given me a very poor quality of life. No one can understand the pressure that I'm going through daily suffering with these constant abusive torments going on inside my entire body. Yes, it's a miracle that I'm still alive as my battle with demons has raged on for well over thirty four years, coping and dealing with this awful affliction.

It's with me everywhere I go. If I'm shopping, in church or talking to friends on the phone, I'm snared and trapped. The privacy of my body and life disappeared once the demon gang got into my life. Could anyone who's reading this book stand living with this condition like I have? Voices and being molested with movements going on non-stop inside of you is very draining. Unclean spirits are an energy without a body. That's why they need to find a body to ensnare and use as a host to carry out their plans of attack on a human victims.

When a demonic stronghold enters the body it gives them full access to the experience of living inside a human which they can use or ruin a person if they choose to do so. These gangs of demons are trained assassins at destroying and killing people if they can. They will continue their path of destruction for as long as they remain inside a person until deliverance occurs. My book is not a fantasy but a true story that happened to me. It became my reality which I've lived with since this anti-Christ event entered me in the 1980s. What's written in the New Testament of the bible about unclean spirits is true and still applies today. Jesus came up against these type of conditions within his ministry and cast demons out of people.

I am a visionary and have clairaudience (clear hearing). Also, I have clear vision and am able to see scenes involving people like a rolling film. I experience this quite often. I don't sit down and meditate, I get visions that just appear to me out of nowhere. Since I've suffered with this condition I've seen many religious visions and many others from everyday life. In the bible, many people heard voices and also saw visions that appeared to them that came from God.

Before my trouble began I was leading a very busy active life as I explained earlier in this book, working in show business. Once this spiritual warfare began attacking my life it became an ongoing battle for me to survive each day. For anyone who becomes a victim of this condition, to live through it and survive to tell the tale is truly a miracle. Once the enemy invaded my body it felt like I was living in a concentration camp from then onwards. I was being held a prisoner against my will in my own body. Demonization for a victim is a sentence of living in a hellish daily condition. The privacy and freedom of your body are lost once the perpetrators from hell move in.

My experience of living with this ongoing horror story has never completely ended. It's been going on without respite for more than thirty four years. This is one of the reasons why I wrote this book, to let people know that my condition is a genuine one that is still happening to many people. It's left me up to the present time still battling with the forces of darkness. These perpetrators originate from Satan and are an army who're well trained to attack the human race. Once a person becomes their victim they have no peace or rest, just ongoing days and nights of torture and torments. The demonic stronghold aims non-stop to corrupt the host. They use the body for their abusive games and make many attempts to control the person by fear. If that doesn't work and the host resists, then they aim at destroying the body with illness. This is what has been happening to me.

Demons thrive on torturing a victim for hours on end using brainwashing so the person can't sleep and this damages the health. This can go on for days until the victim feels that they would be better off dead… that's exactly what the demon has in mind. The affected person begins thinking about suicide as they try to drive him or her nutty with the nightly tortures. I've experienced these type of non-stop days and nights of misery from these residents from hell over the passing years. This made me think that quite a few deaths could have been caused to different people who didn't realize that they were being demonized. Believe me, this fury from hell when it's released into the mind and body can easily cause death. What I'm saying sounds very unbelievable but it's an ongoing horrific torture once demons enter the body.

These tortures are infinitely evil and come from a realm of wickedness that's unexplainable to describe because it's so horrendous. It's not over yet! When more reinforcements of demons arrive from hell in a person's home, then voices may be heard everywhere. The victim sinks into an even deeper state of despair. I've suffered with this ordeal for half of my lifetime and I can confirm it exists. The devil is still alive and working around the clock in the world that we all live in to ruin people's lives. The biblical stories in the New Testament are completely true and demons exist today as they did in Jesus time on Earth. No words can explain how terrifying this ordeal is to bare without going insane. These attacks on the human race are still being done by the principalities from hell.

I've learned to remain steadfast against these tyrant gangs from hell with their oppressive and sadistic tactics that they've used against me up to this moment while I'm typing. It's been a long tough fight to survive Satan's invasion with his army of demons, who're are holding my body in jeopardy until I'm set free. Yes, it's a serious ordeal that will ruin people's chances of having a normal existence or a relationship as it has mine. Who'd believe this horrifying story that I've been forced to live with?

Yes, it's caused me a lot of grief and hardships trying to continue fighting on against this bondage in order to survive. How can I explain or put into words to you what this type of terrorizing does to a person? Every organ inside the body can be physically damaged.   This has already caused me to have two major operations. Once these devils arrive in your life the peace you once knew is gone… it's banished forever! They utilize non-stop physical abuse twenty four hours a day that one can't believe is happening. Where has my life gone? Yes, my world started to disappear once this condition began to materialize. From then on I became a prisoner trying to escape from this hell that came into my body.

My story will appear unbelievable for many people and difficult to understand but it's true and I'm still living with it to a certain degree today. Gangs of demons will cling on to a victim once they find their body to reside in and use. Demons use the wavelengths of the mind to hear every thought then use this to create mischief and trouble with other people in the person's life. Once this horror story is placed inside the body of a recipient it will cause havoc non-stop to ruin their entire world.

Please be very careful if you're hearing voices as they can be devils, not amiable spirits. Always be vigilant. Too many Christians are complacent and think the devil doesn't exist and that it's just a story. He does and he's alive and active in the world and you'll certainly know this is a fact if his gangs of demons come into contact with you.

I'm still fighting on to this very moment even as I write my story. Over the years I've learnt not to show my emotions openly to the outside world as no one's really interested in hearing constantly about the same problem so I say I'm ok. That's part of the reason why I've adapted to dealing with my suffering in my own way. I try to keep a positive outlook and keep myself motivated with things that make me feel better. My journey is still not over and I'm still searching for my Holy Grail of peace and deliverance. What life can I ever have living with demons on a journey of anguish, pain and terrorization? It's taken a great deal of willpower on my part to keep my mind and body functioning each day in my life until I'm finally set free.

Chapter 23

2011 to 2016

Up until 2011 I'd depended solely on the church for help and still hadn't been delivered. It wasn't their fault, it just hadn't happened. I respect the church's views and methods but I still hadn't found my deliverance even though I'd persevered with prayer and kept attending church regularly. Nothing changed a great deal for me and I remained suffering with the condition which can shatter one's faith though I'd managed to hold onto mine throughout my trials. There are very few priests trained to deal with demonization or possession so it's hard to find a local priest who might be able to help with this issue. Many of the people that I've seen never seem to grasp or understand how serious and unnatural this condition is to live with.

My life's on-hold waiting for an answer. In the world we live in people mainly look at the visual appearance of a person and cannot detect what's going on inside a mind or body. That's why people need to see some type of visual proof of irregular behavior like screaming or pulling your hair out or cursing Christ in a crazy manner. If this type of behavior takes place then there's proof that something abnormal is going on. A person can be being attacked at any time in a public place by the demons inside their body and it goes undetected because there is no visual evidence. This helps the demons to continue abusing a person at any time they choose.

I remained hoping that God would come up with a miracle. Why God hasn't answered my prayers has been my endless question. I believe the mind is a very a powerful tool that can heal or destroy us by the way we think. This has kept me holding onto my goal that I will rid myself from this tidal wave of destruction that's engulfed my life since the 1980s.

I've noticed that the demonic stronghold remain silent inside my body hiding when the exorcist is trying to remove them. By doing this they've remained inside my body and continue tormenting me, many times taking me to the verge of suicide. They are masters of playing devious tricks when someone is trying to take them out of the body. For me, the word parasites describes how unclean spirit networks operate. The parasite and demons both drain the human body and bring infections and illness to the body so there's the similarity.

No, I never expect other people to understand what I'm going through as it's my cross to suffer, not theirs. Who truthfully really cares about other people's problems? I've spent half of my life living and putting up with this macabre situation that I'm still going through. Many times the church hasn't brought me hope but overwhelming despair. My condition may be unusual and I agree it is but everything in life has an answer if you search long enough to find one. My life's been devastated enough already so I need to keep a positive outlook to survive and set myself free.

The demonic gangs have played many foul tricks with me to turn me away from Christianity and to stop my prayers. They were able to change pictures that I had of Jesus Christ into perverted images to make me think that Jesus was in some way involved with my tortures. I've also had a variety of realistic images that I believe were religious ones with different types of faces looking at me from the clouds in the sky. There have been a number of visions while I'm watching TV or anywhere I go.

Today I question everything I hear or see and have to deduce whether I want to accept or reject it. This helps me to keep myself sane from horrific apparitions or illusions. Demons are masters of deception and lies. They are experts on how to destroy humans once they gain access to your life. Living with them has taught me to keep searching for an answer to find my freedom. It might take more time but the answer is out there somewhere to eradicate this bondage which has been clinging onto my life for far too long.

My faith has kept me strong in believing that healing has been taking place over the years to keep me alive through all these horrendous trials that I've been through from the enemy. I've no idea of how my final healing or deliverance will take place, only God knows. Sometimes a complete change is needed to set oneself free from the past.

Until what's haunting my body is totally destroyed by the fire of God or a miracle takes place by some other method, I remain still searching for peace in my life and freedom of body and mind. If you ask anybody in general would they like to accept this terrible suffering in their life the answer would be no. Living with this condition has devoured up everything that makes life worth living. I find it hard to believe that God stands by and watches people suffering daily with this type of horrendous condition like I've had for so long? My concept of God is that he shows great mercy and love for his people, that's why I continue praying to him for help.

Chapter 24

Living with the Condition

Luke 11-24:25:26 taken from the holy bible New International Version. NIV

When an evil spirit comes out of a man, it goes through arid places seeking rest and does not find it. Then it says I will return to the house I left. When it arrives it finds the house swept clean and put in order. Then it goes and takes seven other spirits more wicked than itself, and they go in and live there. And the final condition of that man is worse than the first.

In February 2014, I did some research on the internet as my condition was growing progressively worse. While I was searching I found an exorcist in America who appeared to have a great deal of experience in dealing with my type of condition. I called him and arranged an appointment for my first exorcism session by phone. The sessions began and I hoped that they'd finally lead to my deliverance taking place. Generally after each phone session I felt very exhausted because they caused me to bring up bile. This took place when the unclean spirit surfaced and spoke during the session. One evening after one of these sessions, I heard a voice coming from a picture of Jesus that I had on a calendar and it said quite clearly "you won't die." That night when I went to bed I felt as if my life's energy was slipping away from me and that I was about to die. While lying in bed feeling extremely ill, I could still hear the voice of the exorcist in America reminding me that it could take some time to be delivered.

This gave me some hope of being delivered from the nightmare that clung onto my body. That night as I lay dazed and weak in bed, I wondered where the answer lay for me in order to become free. Then I gradually fell into a deep troubled sleep and passed out for a few hours. When I woke up during the night I could hardly lift myself up off the bed. When I tried to stand up I couldn't and had to make a great effort to get my balance. I had to struggle to put one foot in front of the other to walk to the toilet and then get myself a drink. Although I felt very ill after each session, I knew they were helping me understand how to put demons out of action.

I had to remain at home the following day as I was too unwell to go anywhere. I kept hoping that God's intervention would come and remove my ordeal completely through the sessions with the exorcist. Throughout that period I continued praying for the strength to win my battle with the realms of darkness and be victorious in evicting the gang of demons. The phone exorcisms went on for about a year and then ended because the exorcist had too much work and couldn't do them any longer with me. He was very helpful and suggested that I should continue doing exorcisms using his prayer videos that he'd recorded which were on the internet.

Since 2016, I've battled on alone with the condition with my health deteriorating at a rapid pace. The health issues resulted in hospital visits caused by the demonic infestation. During that year I completed my first book. It was published and went out on Amazon in the September of that year... the title of the book being Trials Torments and Teaching. This book is a wonderful example of how Christ can touch people like myself on the Earth. Jesus has the omnipotent power to do this for people who are receptive and sensitive enough to be able to receive and write words down through the Holy Spirit.

I'd never done much writing before my first book and it was an achievement for me because the teachings came through the Holy Spirit during my years of suffering. Living with these ongoing battles of demonic warfare eats up your energy and wellbeing and stops you being able to lead a normal existence. Your life is trapped living in this paranormal world with demons. The condition also left terrible scars on my son as well, having to see me in this condition daily with no apparent solution. My story has been an incredible, almost unexplainable one. We're in 2017 at this moment in time while I'm completing writing this book {Haunted by Demons} and I still haven't found my Holy Grail of deliverance to end my struggles with the realms of darkness.

When I look back on the past and Ankara at the time when Tarik appeared back in my life again, I can see now that he was being used like a pawn in a chess game. We were both being manipulated on the occasion of his entrance at the club that night. It opened the door for the demons to enter and have access to my life. Shortly after his appearance at the club the mischief with the voices began along with my long-term nightmare of horror and trials. We were both used by the devils for the games that they enjoy playing with people's lives. We were placed on their chess board for them to begin their game of interference with mischief and lies. The old serpent had arranged these games and found a way to twist and coil around my marital situation once Tarik came back into my life. From then onwards the venom was spread into my work, family life and health to destroy the entire world that I lived in.

I never knew when all this was taking place that I was a natural medium, visionary and sensitive with the gift of clairvoyance (which means that I'm able to hear spirits). The church class this gift as being a visionary or sensitive. Many times I see things from past ages that are clear and moving images that appear like a rolling film being shown to me. It's a mystery to me how I can pick up a variety of different peoples voices such as movie stars, statesmen and others without making any effort or trying to do so, I just hear them. I never meditate or go into any type of trance as most mediums do. The voices just come without any effort. Living with demon gangs for such a lengthy period of time has taught me to be careful and vigilant about what I'm hearing or seeing. Before my ordeal took place, I'd no knowledge of what unclean spirits or demons could do to people once they become attached to or enter a body. I was totally ignorant until I started learning about the paranormal and supernatural world.

Chapter 25

Imprisoned by Demonization

A metaphor on what I've been through would be to compare my demonization to an infestation of rats or cockroaches in a building. It's an awful ordeal for the owners of the building to cope with but eventually a solution will be found to end the manifestation and the unwelcome guests will be killed off and gone.

From the 1980s my life was swallowed up into living in a strange supernatural world which came from out of nowhere. The experience of living with it since then has been totally shattering and unbelievable for me. In the beginning it was very difficult for me to believe that the ordeal was happening to me, being quite a logical person myself. Once this supernatural spiritual warfare began my world began disappearing within a short space of time. The years that followed were engulfed with intensive trials of torments which I've already described. Throughout those years I never stopped searching for help and looking for answers to rid myself of this ongoing haunting of my body. I've spent years living with the imprisonment of this condition trying to escape from it.

The journey's been a non-stop and horrifying one for me which has given me a poor quality of life having to live and cope with these ongoing attacks being done to me as I've grown older with the passing years. I've continued praying daily to God for my deliverance and remained steadfast in doing this over the years. I'm dreading the prospect of spending the rest of the days that I have left living with this abomination. It's left me desperately waiting for an answer from God to end my hellish state.

It's easy for you to guess where the title of my first book came from {Trials Torments and Teachings} which was written while I was on my journey with the residents from hell. I'm just one of the many people who're suffering with this type of condition in England. People are too frightened of being labelled mentally disturbed or schizophrenic if they mention that they're suffering with hearing voices or being molested by an unknown force. These acts are being done to people and carried out by the demonic spirits in gangs. Individual people continue to suffer in silence because they're too ashamed to come forward and talk about their problem because this condition creates a stigma. It's not an everyday issue but a supernatural one. That's hard for the public to grasp and understand. This is a major problem for the victims who're living and suffering with these types of attacks.

If a victim does pluck up courage to seek help from the medical profession, they have very little knowledge or understanding about these type of issues or what causes them. The symptoms of both possession and demonization are similar to mental disorders but are not. A victim must be very careful otherwise he or she can end up being labelled a mental case by a doctor's diagnosis and end up in a mental ward. I've met other people who're having demonic attacks and I know it's still going on as it did in Jesus time when he lived on the Earth... it's existed since time began. People are waiting for the chains of these conditions to be broken and to be set free.

I'm still waiting to get my life back on track and completely free from this soul-destroying and unnatural condition and its bondage. It takes away your freedom and the privacy in your life. These parasites will draw the last bit of energy and life out of a person's body as long as they remain inside it to maim a victim.

Demonization is a destructive and demoralizing energy that wants to take every positive aspect and action out of a person's life and turn it into a negative one of despair and hopelessness so that you'll never be set free. If anyone who's reading my book is having this type of experience, I'd like you to remember me in your darkest hours. I've been there too and I might be able to help you. Do aim at keeping a positive outlook so you survive and live through this horrendous ordeal from the pits of hell. I'm a Christian who's spent half of my life time trying to rid myself from being terrorized by demons. It's been a long ongoing battle fighting on daily which no-one would believe that's given me days and nights without sleep and ill health.

I agree that my story is stranger than fiction and might appear difficult for sceptics to believe. Looking at my appearance you'd never guess what I've suffered and been through for so many years. Many people don't believe that these type of paranormal encounters exist or are still going on. Everything that I've written in this book comes from my own experience and knowledge of having lived with this type of phenomenon. This is not fake or a scam, it's completely true and describes what I've had to tolerate and live with. I've come out of the closet with my story to tell people the truth to give them a deep insight about the enigma of demonization with this book. Yes, it's hard to comprehend or understand why these types of acts of evil warfare take place to ruin people's lives. All I can tell you is that it's definitely an anti-Christ activity... that's my answer.

People make wild guesses as to why these supernatural phenomena take place, even science has no explanation or answer for them. This leaves us with the question 'why'? Demons are an energy without a body who're programmed to create havoc in anyone's life that they touch or come into contact with. They're trained experts at planting lies and treachery into the mind of any victim. This can be applied to innocent people that the demons find ways of ensnaring and attacking through no fault of their own.

Remember these words if you ever hear voices, they might be from these types of perpetrators, so be on your guard. They are an enemy and not friendly spirits as I thought at first when I heard them. They come from the pit and bring nothing but damage and havoc into a person's life. If you can imagine having a boa constrictor squeezing the life out of you then clinging on to ruin your entire body and existence, that's what they do. Demonic strongholds are very dangerous to live with once they get a hold. On top of everything else, living in this situation and staying alive is a totally mind-blowing traumatic experience to deal with Now I totally believe the stories in the New Testament completely about Jesus casting devils out of people and setting them free. Those stories are not fantasy but were real being caused by Satan's networks of demons who're still roaming the Earth. Everything in this book did actually happen to me throughout the years.

Chapter 26

Summarizing How I Feel

It's been a long weary journey over the years trying to resolve my problem with demonization that's shattered my existence, causing me to search for an answer to set myself free. Many of the people whom I've met claimed to have the answer but none of them did. This has left me living in a limbo type of existence between a supernatural world and my own. It's gradually drained my life away since Turkey in the 1980s as its continued on over the passing years without respite. I've had no choice but to adjust myself to dealing with it the best I can until I'm set free.

My condition is an unusual one for other people to believe and understand. In the near future I hope that I'll be able to help other people who might be suffering with this type of issue in their lives. It causes overwhelming amounts of mental and physical trauma for anyone suffering with it. Where can you turn to for help to discuss this type of issue? It can be difficult to find the right person who will stick with you until you are set free.

My book is based on true events that I've had to deal with for many years. Every person's case is different and arrives through a different set of circumstances. The victim may have similar signs or symptoms not unlike those I've experienced. My story is stranger than fiction and a supernatural one that I've come out of the closet to tell. People who've suffered with various types of this condition are generally too frightened to talk about it in public. That's why I'm revealing the true facts with this book based on what I've experienced, having lived with this ordeal in my life.

For the past few years I've been demoralized with brainwashing by the perpetrators with torments being inflicted upon me for being an older person now, insinuating that I'll never find happiness or freedom as it's too late. If you're a sensitive like I am and can hear all these terrible torments daily, it's totally soul-destroying to live with. Having this oppression in my life has left me wondering how I've survived throughout the years living with this misery every day in my life.

Throughout the past years I've been living a cliffhanger existence searching for an answer to set myself free. In Ankara it took me a lengthy time to recognize what I was actually suffering with. Once I knew what the condition was inside my body, it was terrifying for me to deal with. My stigma had begun and the peace and freedom of my body and life had gone. I'm a sensitive and the gift of being one has become an endless curse in my life over time.

Throughout the years I've studied and learnt a lot more about the condition which made me realize that a lot of people are suffering in silence who have it. They may not even be aware that the condition has become part of their lifestyle. That's why I hope this book will give people some idea of what the condition of demonization is like if it touches a person's life. This supernatural intervention can take place in people of any age or gender and I'm living proof of that.

Usually this type of condition is only discussed behind closed doors by afflicted people who decline from discussing it publicly because the issue holds a social stigma. Remember my words… demons, unclean spirits or evil spirits are all perpetrators of destruction for any victim they ensnare. Their perverted attacks are carried out and done to men, women and children in gangs. If you're a sceptic or a non-believer who doesn't believe what I'm saying is true, it's up to you. Maybe people who read my book might think that I'm nuts or looking for publicity, well you can think what you like. I've lived with this hellish state and know that it exists. In the New Testament of the bible, Jesus cast out these unclean spirits from people with his ministry.

Once demons gained entrance into my body they had easy access to gaining information about my character and life. Having this connection with me gave other unclean spirits the facility to come and join the gang to torment me. When more demonic spirits came later they filled my home with voices talking around my house non-stop. This started to drive me nuts when it manifested. The scenario of it is mind blowing with its effects that can last for days. Ghosts and demons can reside outside or inside a body and also be attached to a person.

After having lived with demons for years I can tell you that it's a horrific affliction of daily torture with no escape which gradually makes you think that there's no other way out for you but death to end your misery. This scenario is what the stronghold of demons want. Then the Grim Reaper appears and waits at the door of death in anticipation of you passing through it. I've reached this point many times through the misery and hopelessness that this type of bondage brings to your life. It's a totally soul-destroying experience that's held my life in jeopardy.

Demons enjoy applying sadistic tortures to their victims and abusing every orifice in their body to damage and maim them. Their brainwashing is pure evil venom aimed at destroying a victim mentally with their sadistic trials while inside the body they try to ruin the anatomy. Having this abomination inside your body will cause post-traumatic stress disorder (PTSD) which people get when they are put under constant traumatic stressful situations.

Now I understand what soldiers must suffer and go through in war zones being confronted daily with horrendous ordeals and having to put up with them. The constant battering of being a victim of a demonic gang can quite easily drive a person insane or suicidal. I've been through these trials and tortures and they can drive you right over the edge. Demonic spirits are masters at what they do. They studied at The Pits of Hell College.

My ongoing advice to anyone who might start hearing voices is… be on your guard and test what you're hearing, ask questions and get help. If you've suddenly started hearing strange voices who aren't from the people around you, be very careful. Demonic spirits are very clever and will begin by being friendly to see if you respond. Be vigilant as you might be hearing one of Satan's assassins looking for a host to live in. If it's a demonic gang it'll be a field-day when they move in, interfering with your body and life using their games of never-ending abuse and destruction. Demons are experts at what they do, ruining and corrupting people's lives in the world that we live in.

When I look back over the years of my life since the 1980s they all seem to have been swallowed up through living with the residents from hell in a strange supernatural world. For me it's been a solitary journey of internment with this conflict until it comes to an end. Ever since it arrived I've been imprisoned within my own body. It engulfed my normal life with terrifying supernatural ordeals of horror. With suffering trials that consumed my body and life into the realms of darkness and despair. When the enemy arrived with his cohorts to cause havoc with spiritual warfare in my life.

With the majority of stories about hauntings of building or places there's generally a reason why the ghost hasn't stopped haunting the place and needs to be looked into by a priest or again someone who has experience and knowledge to end this haunting. It's the same with devils, demons or unclean spirits as these are just different terms that are used for the same demonic who might be haunting a body which is similar, only now when it's in a human body it causes a great deal more conflict like I've experienced living with the condition. For any person living with this condition it creates a certain amount of fear and because it's coming from an unknown alien force living inside you which is abnormal and unexplainable. Which will create a state of hopelessness for any victim having to live with this ordeal daily, as it has for me without being set free. Every moment of my life is filled with the stress of having to deal with my situation each day. Having this boa constrictor ruining my health and squeezing my life away.

Chapter 27

My Life Today

"For I know the plans I have for you" declares the Lord. "Plans to prosper you and not to harm you, plans to give you hope and a future. Then you will call upon me and come and pray to me, and I will listen to you. You will seek me and find me when you seek me with all your heart." Jeremiah 29:11-13 "NIV" taken from the Holy Bible.

Everything that I've written comes from my experience of being held a prisoner with demonization. Networks of demons are still in existence and using people's bodies as hosts to dwell in. Having this supernatural invasion in my life has left lasting effects from the condition which I'm still having to deal with up to the present time. The worse part of the condition is losing one's privacy of your own body and coping with the mental and physical abuse that the condition causes. Living at close quarters with demonic spirits is a shattering experience which I've had to handle since it began that have left me feeling very isolated many times and suffering alone. There are quite a few people who don't believe that this type of supernatural ordeal is still taking place and happening to people. This affliction of the body is invisible which means that you're walking on that tightrope daily with it in your life while you continue to suffer with it.

When I read newspaper headlines now that are due to unknown circumstances it really makes me wonder because demonization can go undetected and easily lead a victim to the point of committing suicide. That's why unresolved strange cases of people's deaths interest me and what caused them. Could it be what I've been suffering with because it's a plague once it comes into your life to destroy you if it can? It leads me think that demonic gangs could be attacking many people where there's sudden death or when suicide takes place where there's no logical reason.

Deaths can also take place through a person's vice which demons will use to gain a foothold into the person's life. The individual will be totally unaware of what's happening as they have already lost control with the vice they have. This leaves the door open for the demons to enter and manifest to create terrible afflictions of depression and hopelessness that could lead to suicide through demonic oppression and bondage.

I've found many similarities between demons and vampires in the way that they use their victims. A vampire draws blood out its victim's body that leaves the person in a lifeless state. Demons attack a victim non-stop which ruins the immune system and creates illness, leaving the victim lacking in energy and lifeless. Both of these ordeals create the body to malfunction and create disease.

The bombardment from these type of attacks are highly dangerous to live with and cause traumatic stress and ill health for any victim. Speaking from my own experience, its taken great endurance for me to bare and survive since it materialized into my life. From then on it has been an ongoing roller coaster ride for me that's kept going throughout the years, destroying everything that I attempt to achieve that would bring happiness and achievement into my life.

During this year I've grown a lot frailer due to the ongoing trials which are still going on. They have caused a great deal of deterioration in my body with health issues. Living daily with these supernatural torments of molestation is very hard to explain to the average person who wouldn't have a clue as to what I'm talking about. These types of unclean spirits can remain hidden, residing inside a body for years until the person is finally set free. This means that the victim's tortures will continue endlessly. It is an atrocious ordeal to live with from the pits of hell. The whole condition has swallowed up the best years of my life since it began haunting my body.

When my story began I was working in show business as an all-round trained dancer and singer with my own shows. I was a fit person until the powers of darkness arrived with their tactics to create havoc and oppression in my life in order to gain control over my body. Then my normal life that I had in show business turned into a full blown horror story. From then on, I became a hostage of the rulers of darkness. Their invisible chains bound me and stopped me being able to live my life to its full capacity. Although I keep my daily suffering well-hidden from everyone around me and seem to be coping well, some days I have overwhelming bouts of despair through being held by these chains of bondage and oppression in my life.

My son still lives with me and knows the horrors that I've been through living with the condition over the years that broke our family up. I ask you… who wants to live with this type of existence? I understand now how people lose their faith which I've come close to doing many times. I've struggled on praying and hoping for a miracle to be set free from my unbearable situation. Yes, I've wondered many times why God hasn't delivered me in my darkest hours of despair and hopelessness living with the demonization while it pounded my mind and body for hours on end. Yet throughout all these times I've held onto my faith and belief in God.

Despite these thoughts filtering through my mind and through all the worst moments that I've experienced, I've never let go of my goal to set myself free and never stopped fighting for my freedom. I'll continue doing this until my final breath if that's what it takes. Looking at my life today, it has changed a great deal from the one that I had working in show business when my story began. Over the years it's had moments when it seemed to be turning into a Greek tragedy. I'm still anticipating a happy ending to my story and to regaining my body and life back so I'll be able to spend the rest of my years peacefully.

Living with this condition has been equivalent to serving a long-term prison sentence that's restricted my life. Not wanting to involve other people with my problem is part of the reason why I never remarried. During 2015 I battled on endlessly with the anti-Christ against all odds and completed my first book with the help of the Holy Spirit towards the end of the year. And the book is out on Amazon - titled Trials Torments and Teaching.

My ongoing question over the years has been... why did this nightmare happened to me that turned my world upside down? Demonization and possession are both enigmas that are generally kept well hidden from the public when they take place. That's what made me determine to come out of the closet with my story and tell the truth with this book. From my point view as a victim who's suffered with it for half of my lifetime. I want to give the public a deeper insight into the truth about the condition with my story of what happened to me. not with someone else's view on the subject who has never experienced this type of horrendous ordeal. I've been unable to escape from this ongoing nightmare and learnt to live my life the best way I can keeping my secret well hidden from the outside world.

I believe these attacks came partly because I'm a Christian and I believe in God, so I was an ideal target for attack. When my issue began, I had a successful career in show business and a stable family life. During the years that I worked in show business with my husband's orchestras and with our variety shows around the world, we were respected everywhere we worked and had no major problems. This continued until the 1980s when the spiritual hosts of wickedness arrived on the scene and the demonization began in my life. From then onwards a tidal wave of destruction swept over my life that gradually took everything away that I held dear, leaving me with the condition of being haunted by demonic gangs on a regular basis.

While I've been completing the last few chapters, there's been the usual interference and retaliation going on against me for writing this book. Satan doesn't want the information that I'm writing to be spread to the public as it reveals his agenda for his attacks on the human race and strictly 'private'. I'm finishing this book in the room looking over the garden where I started my story. Its walls are embedded with many eerie tales that took place right here, in this room. I'm tired after having spent countless years trying to eliminate the demons from my life that have left me still searching for the answer as to the means of banishing the remnants of them forever.

Living with the residents from hell has been a traumatic experience for me and my first book's title conveys everything in three words with its title... Trials Torments and Teachings. My journey with the rulers of darkness confirmed to me that they exist along with their boss Lucifer who is still recruiting and sending armies of evil spirits to attack humans on Earth with all types of evil warfare like I've experienced. The hymn Onward Christian Soldiers seems to say it all. 'Marching on to war' has been an ongoing endless battle of mine throughout the years. I've been fighting on throughout each day to regain my body and life back and to survive the devil's evil wiles. Everything that I've written comes from the first-hand knowledge that I've gained over the years of being attacked by demonic gangs who are trained enlisted armies of assassins sent to attack the human race.

My aim is to open people's eyes to the fact that the devil is alive and among us, working overtime night and day to corrupt, tempt and ruin lives. Read and digest my words and open your ears and listen to my information. God's also working twenty four hours a day to crush the serpent and his acts against the human race. Although I might appear to be nuts, I'm hoping that this book might pave the way for people to get more help for those who might be suffering with this condition in their life. I didn't make up this story it happened to me and took place in my own life. I would categorize the condition as a hellish state and a night terror that you can't wake up from once it begins. .

Don't play around with demons... they're not here on Earth to play games. They're here for the kill! The only game they like playing is the one that leads to your destruction and death. Take heed of my words and don't call demons up! All demonic spirits are trained assassins in deception by the father of lies himself… trained to achieve their task and to ensnare victims into their trap.

My life today is very different from the one that I had when my story began so long ago in Ankara. Today I'm frequently on social media and also running a friendship prayer group… and hope to continue writing. Once this book is published there will be many sceptics waiting to argue about my condition, looking for proof of how I've survived such horrific ordeals to tell my story. Other people might consider me to be a complete nutter or someone who's looking for publicity. I'm neither, I assure you. The public are completely justified to have their own opinions about my story.

Always remain vigilant and once again remember my words… the enemy is everywhere we go and with many of the people we meet and mix with. He's amongst us waiting to ensnare and trap victims with all their favorite indulgency's that we all love so much! Be on your guard!

My aim is to promote myself with various talks with the purpose of helping other people who might be suffering with the condition. I hope one day in the future there will be   another book with the testimony of what happened to me next that finally set me free and changed my life. Who has the answer and the key to close the door into the supernatural world and finally set me free?

Someone holds the answer to end my prison sentence and liberate me from my endless nightmare. Who?